"Aieee-ye-ye-ye!"

Sands' head jerked to the right. A cry tore from his throat before he located the source of that blood-curdling scream. "Ambush!"

The warning drowned in a chorus of war cries that rent the air. From both sides, mounted Comanches, their faces painted in the reds and blacks of war, drove their ponies down on the patrol. In one glance, Sands knew he had underestimated the raiding party. At least seventy Comanches howled about him.

Sands heard the sickening thud of an arrow striking solid flesh. Beside him, a man desperately clawed at his back, trying to dislodge the Comanche shaft that jutted there. Then he tumbled from the saddle.

All this Sands saw and comprehended before his mind gave a name to the man at his side—Shorty Green. Sands had shared breakfast with the man that morning. Now . . .

THE TEXIANS

ZACH WYATT

PINNACLE BOOKS NEW YORK

ATTENTION: SCHOOLS AND CORPORATIONS

PINNACLE Books are available at quantity discounts with bulk purchases for educational, business or special promotional use. For further details, please write to: SPECIAL SALES MANAGER, Pinnacle Books, Inc., 1430 Broadway, New York, NY 10018.

This is a work of fiction. All the characters and events portrayed in this book are fictional, and any resemblance to real people or incidents is purely coincidental.

THE TEXIANS

Copyright © 1984 by Geo. W. Proctor

All rights reserved, including the right to reproduce this book or portions thereof in any form.

An original Pinnacle Books edition, published for the first time anywhere.

First printing/May 1984

ISBN: 0-523-42219-9

Can. ISBN: 0-523-43211-9

Cover illustration by Bruce Minney

Printed in the United States of America

PINNACLE BOOKS, INC.
1430 Broadway
New York, New York 10018

9 8 7 6 5 4 3 2 1

*To the original H.A.C.s Neal Barrett, Warren Norwood,
and Pierce Watters.*

THE TEXIANS

★ONE★

Joshua Sands hated the night . . . the waiting.

His anxious disquiet stemmed from his patrol duty along the frontier of the San Antonio region. Like any ranger, he cursed the long hours in the saddle, the hundreds of fruitless trails, the unpredictable Texas weather, the rocky terrain, and the cold camps. But they were bearable. The night and the waiting were an eternity unto themselves that a man endured each twenty-four hours.

An impatient sigh worked free from deep within Sands' chest as he rolled on his back. Gazing at the star-sprinkled sky, he tried to forget the Comanche raiding party whose trail the patrol had followed for two days. There was no assurance the Indians still ran before them. Comanches had the habit of circling back on pursuers when least expected, turning the hunter into the hunted.

Sands reached inside his coat to dig two fingers into the breast pocket of his buckskin shirt and pulled out a gold watch. He thumbed it open. The moonlight played across its face. A quarter to midnight, fifteen minutes until he had to relieve young Willard Brown from the night watch—an additional four sleepless hours atop those he had just tossed through.

Snapping the timepiece shut, he ran his fingertips over the intricately engraved design ornamenting the case. A rider in full English fox hunting attire clung low to his mount's neck as the horse bounded over a hedgerow.

Irony twisted the corners of the ranger's mouth. The pocket watch once belonged to his mother's great grandfather, a Cornish country squire. Civilized gentlemen chasing fox were a far cry from tracking Comanche across the arid Texas hill country.

Sands tried to recall his mother's stories about her family's journey from England to Tennessee. His memories failed him. His only vivid recollections of his twenty-two years were of Texas. He could not imagine the Tennessee hills, let alone the English countryside.

With a wistful shake of his head, Sands sat up. He neatly rolled and tied the blanket that had covered him. The night's chill edged deeper into his body. Rippling waves of gooseflesh moved up his back and down his arms. The bite of the night, or apprehension? He did not know.

Methodically, he checked the single-shot pistols tucked in his belt, then lifted a cap and ball rifle from the ground beside him to give it the same careful attention. The rifle was his pride, hand-crafted by a Mexican gunsmith in Corpus Christi. In five years, the weapon had never failed to fire. A fact that meant the difference between life and death when facing a charge from war-painted, howling Comanches. The brace of pistols and the rifle gave him three shots before having to reload.

Finally his right hand reached down to touch the familiar handle of a long, wide-bladed hunting knife slung on his hip. The knife was smaller than the legendary blade Jim Bowie had carried. True Bowie knives were a rarity, in spite of numerous claims to the contrary by traveling weapons salesmen.

The ten-inch blade, honed to a razor-sharp cutting edge, scabbarded at his waist was enough for Sands' purposes. He had proved that on several occasions when three shots had not been enough to drive off attacking Indians.

The knife was also balanced for throwing, half a turn every six feet. Although, Sands thought, only a fool would throw a knife in hand-to-hand fighting. Once a blade was tossed, a man was weaponless and as good as dead.

Pulling the collar of his coat high about his neck and drawing a wide-brimmed hat low to his face, Sands tucked the sleeping roll under an arm and stood. The eighteen other men on the ground around him did not stir. He smiled, wishing he had their ability to push thought from the mind and sleep. If lucky, he might be able to grab a few hours of shut-eye after he was relieved at four.

Weaving quietly among the sleeping men, Sands worked to a clump of willows growing on the bank of a shallow creek that skirted the edge of the camp. Twenty horses, saddled for action, stood tied to the drooping branches.

Sands gave his silent approval. Jack Hays, his captain, was a natural-born Indian fighter. Though but twenty-three years old and a native of Tennessee, Hays had an uncanny grasp of his enemy. He learned all he could about Comanche lore from his Lipan Apache Scouts, then used that knowledge against the Comanches.

The constantly saddled mounts were one of Hays' innovations for ranger patrols—one directly taken from the enemy. It was an old Comanche raiding party trick to keep ponies ready for a hard ride in case of unexpected danger. Hays' men now kept their mounts in the same state of readiness. A simple measure to be certain, but no white man had even considered it before Captain Jack Hays!

Turning from the horses, Sands climbed the water-and-wind-eroded gully that rose fifteen feet above the creek.

Willard Brown sat on a jagged outcropping of limestone, partially concealed by scrub cedar growing around the boulder.

"Midnight," Sands whispered when he reached the youth's position. "Best get some rest. Sun'll be up before you know it."

Willard slid from the rocky perch to allow the older ranger access to the boulder. Sands tossed his sleeping roll atop the limestone then scrambled up to sit on the makeshift cushion.

"Blood Moon." Willard stood, his head craned back to stare at the full moon overhead. "Josh, is it always like this? Do you get used to it?"

"Never . . . just learn to accept it." Sands understood the seventeen-year-old's unrest. All Texians did. When the full moon hung over the land, Comanche raiding parties rode, smearing blood on the moon in their wake.

Sands eased a pouch of bourbon-soaked tobacco from a coat pocket. He stuffed a pinch into his mouth and slowly chewed. He preferred a pipe, but when ranging, it was too dangerous. The flame from a match could be seen for miles in this open country. He offered the young man the pouch.

Willard waved the tobacco away. "I thought the Comanche didn't ride in the winter. What are they doing raiding in early January?"

"The name of the month doesn't mean it's winter in Texas. You know that." Sands spat a stream of tobacco that looked ink black in the frosty moonlight. "Winter's been too mild. Until a blue norther sweeps down and puts ice on that stream, the Comanches will keep raiding."

"It feels like winter to me." Willard rubbed his arms to increase the circulation.

Sands didn't argue. It was cold, but not winter cold. Eighteen forty was seven days old, and the new decade had yet to see its first freeze. When the ice and perhaps snow came, the raids would stop . . . until Spring. Then the Blood Moon would rise over Texas once more. Sands spat another thin stream of tobacco juice.

"How long you been ranging, Josh?" Willard still stared at the moon.

"Off and on for seven years," Sands replied. "Joined Johnson's ranging company when I was fifteen. Been riding against the Lipans, Tonkawas, Cherokee, and Comanche whenever there's been a call for rangers."

"This is my first time . . . my first patrol," Willard said softly.

"You're pulling your weight like any other man in the company." Sands remembered his first ride and his own lack of confidence. "But if you don't get some sleep, you won't be worth a tinker's dam in the morning."

"I guess you're right . . ." The youth's words faltered. His head jerked to the right, upstream.

Sands heard it too. Splashing water! His thumb eased back the hammer of his rifle. The sound moved closer. The older ranger spat his chaw to the ground.

"Could be an animal . . . antelope or deer," Willard offered while Sands slipped from the outcropping.

"Could be. Only one way to find out." Sands motioned for the young man to follow him to the creek.

For a moment, Sands considered waking the other men, then discarded the idea. If it were Comanches, there were no more than one or two of them. The splashing was not loud enough for a large raiding party. Willard might be right. It could be an animal. Deer were plentiful in this region of Central Texas.

The woman stumbled into view before the two men reached the willows.

Sands froze in mid-stride, his jaw sagging wide. The

woman was totally naked, her bare skin glowing ghostly pale in the moonlight.

"My God!" Willard voiced Sands own surprise. "It's a white woman!"

The woman swirled around to face the two men. She screamed, her voice high-pitched and panicked. Her hands flew out as though to fend off an attack as she stumbled back through the chilling water. She screamed again. Her feet went out from under her. Hands flailing the air for nonexistent support, she tumbled into the creek.

Sands tossed his rifle to Willard and covered the distance to the stream in two strides of his long legs. The woman regained her footing before he reached her. She spun about in a feral crouch to face him.

"Nooooooo!" The single word came in a sibilant growl. Without warning, she lunged forward, hands raised like taloned claws aimed for the ranger's eyes. "I'll kill you! Kill you!"

Sands deftly ducked beneath one raking arm and grabbed the other with his left hand. Simultaneously, his right swung upward. A sharp crack echoed through the gully when his open palm smacked smartly against her cheek.

The woman whimpered, jerked back rigidly, and stared at the ranger in disbelief. Her eyes went wide and round. "You're . . . you're . . . white!"

Before he could reply, she collapsed in his arms, her body flaccid, then shuddering in violent spasms. Her tears came in an uncontrollable flood.

Awkwardly aware of her nakedness, Sands held her as she pressed herself tightly against him. Her diminutive body was almost lost beside his lanky six-foot frame. He did his best to provide what comfort and protection he could. Soothing words fled his mind. All he could do was stroke the gentle curve of her back and repeat over and over. "It's all right now. You're safe."

"Josh, what the hell are you doing? That creek's cold!"

Sands glanced over his shoulder. Jack Hays and the rest of the patrol stood at the water's edge.

"Bring her here before she catches the croup!" Jack waved the ranger from the water.

Maneuvering the sobbing woman toward the bank, Sands heard Jack break his own rule about cold camps by ordering Hap Ingram to light a fire. The ranger captain threw a blanket around the woman's shoulder when Sands led her from the creek. Somehow, without ever releasing her clinging arm from Sands' waist, she managed to wrap the blanket about to conceal her nudity.

While Jack called for someone to brew coffee, Sands edged the woman through the rangers toward the beginning flickers of a campfire. Willard Brown spread a bed roll before the flames and Sands seated his ward atop it. When he tried to step away, she clutched at his arm with a desperate strength. He did not question her grasping need for human contact, but squatted beside her on the blanket.

"Beeman, Williamson, Grant, Utley, and Wayne . . . spread out around the camp. Keep your eyes open. If there's a Comanche within ten miles, this fire'll draw him like a candle bug to a flame," Jack shouted as he lowered himself to the woman's opposite side.

"This ain't coffee, but it might help her some."

Hank Ferris' bearded face appeared to Sands' right. The man held out a tin cup. The distinctive odor of sour mash whiskey invaded Sands' nostrils.

"Ma'am, try drinking this." Jack took the cup and placed it in one of the woman's delicate hands. "It's strong, but it will make you feel a mite better . . . and warmer."

Tears still streaming down her cheeks, the woman's

head lifted. She gazed blankly at the ranger captain, then turned questioningly to Sands. He nodded. Lips tentatively touching the cup's rim, she took a deep drink.

Abruptly, her crying ended. A startled gasp rasped from her throat, followed by an equally surprised chorus of hacking coughs. Jack patted her back and grinned. Her eyes narrowed.

"It's not sherry meant for the refined taste of womenfolk, but it will help," he assured her. "See if you can finish it."

She sucked in a steadying breath and sipped. Bit by bit, she managed to down the whiskey and handed the empty cup back to the captain. She looked at Sands, then Hays. "Who are you?"

"John Coffee Hays, ma'am." The ranger leader touched the brim of his hat. "These men are rangers under my command. We're out of San Antonio."

She sat motionless, staring at the growing fire as though Jack's words had not penetrated her mind. Then she nodded solemnly.

Sands studied her face in the flickering light of the campfire. The ghostly whiteness of her skin had vanished as the whiskey brought a slight blush to her cheeks. She appeared younger than he had originally estimated. Twenty, twenty-two, he decided. Despite the dirt and scratches covering her face, she was pretty.

He imagined her hair clean and soft rather than wet and plastered to her head. It would be long, silky, and as red as the flames warming her. He guessed her height at five feet six inches. And as to what was hidden beneath her makeshift blanket-robe, he didn't have to guess. A handsome woman in any man's eyes.

A thousand questions crowded Sands' mind. What was she doing out here alone? And naked? A woman like this had to have a man. Women, even mud-ugly ones, did not remain single long in Texas, especially on the frontier. There were too many men hungry for a woman. Each one with tongues adangling, aching for a woman to share his life and bed, to bear him sons and daughters.

Sands' head moved slowly from side to side. No man in his right mind would leave a woman alone in this country. No man that was a man.

"Ma'am?" Hank Ferris poked his whiskered face around Hays. This time he held a steaming cup of coffee. "Ain't making no claims as to the taste, but it's coffee and it's hot. It'll take the chill off."

The woman's hand rose to accept the cup. It stopped halfway there, fingers trembling. Her eyes went wide and wild. Her head twisted to Sands. Desperation tautened the features of her face. Both hands grabbed the ranger's arm, digging in like vises.

"Jamie! My baby!" She screamed at him, renewed tears flowing from her green eyes. "They killed my baby, and they've got Jamie! You've got to save him. You've got to save him before they kill him too!"

"Jamie? They?" Sands asked gently, wanting anwers, but afraid of edging her into hysteria again.

"Jamie . . . my son . . . four years old," she answered between sobs. "Comanches have him . . . they killed baby Sara . . . she was crying too loudly . . . one of them picked her up by a leg and swung her head against . . ."

She broke down again, her whole body quaking violently as she buried her face in her hands and wept.

Between Sands' comforting arms and Hays' gentle reassurances that the patrol would do all that was possible to save her captive son, she quieted once more and accepted the coffee. For several minutes, she sipped in silence.

Sands watched her carefully. He saw the transformation—

a determined strength she gathered in preparation to recount what she would rather forget.

"My name is Marion Hammer. Felix, my husband, and I made camp upstream about a half hour before sundown. They rode over a rise and were on us before we knew they were there." She paused, her voice quavering. She took another scalding sip to hold back threatening tears. "There were eight in all . . . faces painted red and black . . . and screaming at the top of their lungs. One of them ran Felix through with a lance as he tried to get his rifle from the wagon."

"What about the others?" Jack asked.

"The others?" She looked at him as though she did not comprehend his meaning.

"The people in the other wagons," he said. "Were they killed too?"

She shook her head. "There were no other wagons. We were alone. Felix had a job offer in El Paso bank. He could speak Spanish. He was college educated."

Book learning or not, Felix Hammer had been a fool, Sands thought. No man traveled the frontier alone or endangered his family by leading them unprotected through Comanche territory. A man invited disaster if he did—the type of disaster that had struck the Hammer family. And like most foolish men, Felix Hammer's mistakes hurt more than just himself.

"Two of them grabbed me and held me on the ground while a third tore my clothes . . ." Marion Hammer's mouth drew closed in a tight, thin line.

There was no need for further details. Among themselves, the Comanches did not permit rape to exist. But they used captive women, white or red. Mrs. Hammer had been taken eight times by her captors, Sands realized, if not more. That she still lived was a miracle. Comanche raiding parties normally eviscerated older female captives when their lust was spent, laughing at the women's dying agonies.

Marion Hammer eventually took a deep breath and began again. After killing her infant daughter, apparently because the child's cries annoyed a brave, they ransacked the wagon.

"They found a few gold pieces and a jug of whiskey Felix had brought along for medicinal purposes," she said.

She described how the braves had stoked the fire for the night, then spread buffalo robes on the ground and passed the jug between them until it was drained, and they were in a drunken stupor.

"One of them took Jamie and made him lie beneath one of the robes with him. They left me sitting there cold and unprotected. I suspect they didn't think I would try anything." She paused again to sip the coffee.

Sands did not question her evaluation of the situation. The braves were probably confident a white woman would be helpless in the desolation of the hill country. That Marion Hammer escaped her captors bespoke of a courage not immediately apparent when looking at the delicate woman.

"I remembered Felix mentioning there were settlements to the south of the camp. When the braves fell asleep, I ran for help," she continued. "I followed the stream until I found you."

Jack poured her another cup of the pan-brewed coffee. "How far do you think you ran?"

She shook her head. "I ran for about four hours. I was afraid to stop . . . afraid they might be following me."

Captain Hays sat motionless for several long moments as though he absorbed and sorted through all she had said, then he turned to his men. "Mrs. Hammer needs clothing and food. See what you can rustle up for her."

The men scattered, moving to the horses and their saddlebags. Minutes later they returned with a wide assortment of proffered clothing in various degrees of cleanliness.

Marion Hammer accepted a pair of pants from Shorty Green and one of Willard Brown's store-bought, flannel shirts. A pair of moccasins taken by one of the men as a souvenir of a previous patrol served in the place of shoes.

Accustomed to Hays' cold-camp rule, the rangers' had little to offer in the way of foodstuffs and variety was non-existent—hardtack and venison jerky. Marion Hammer accepted a portion of each. Her action apparently stemmed from politeness rather than hunger. Sands noted she ate neither.

Jack gathered the men by the fire again and directed Mrs. Hammer to the willows. Blanket clutched about her, she rose and walked into the veiling shadows.

Sands followed, then averted his eyes when he realized her intentions. He felt a strange emptiness within him. For the first time since Marion Hammer stumbled into camp, she did not cling to him. He sucked at his teeth, unable to fathom his reaction to that brief period of dependency on him.

"I want to thank you and your men for their kindness," she said when she returned dressed in the borrowed clothing.

"Thank my men when we get your son back," Jack said as he spread another bed roll in front of the fire for her.

Without hesitation, she stretched atop the blanket and covered herself with the one she carried. Sands watched her, attempting to pair such an able and clear-thinking woman with such a fool as Felix Hammer. He could not understand, nor would he ever comprehend, the method women employed to select a husband. Whatever feminine mystery moved her to choose Felix Hammer, it had been wrong. A fact she would never be able to forget.

For several minutes, he could see her fighting sleep, then the whiskey and exhaustion won out. The tension gripping her facial muscles relaxed; her breathing shallowed to a steady gentle rhythm.

Sands stood and glanced at Jack who motioned him from the sleeping woman's side. "How far you reckon a woman in that shape could travel in four hours?"

"Another woman wouldn't have tried what she did." Sands shrugged. "Even moving barefoot and naked down that cold creek, I don't think we should underestimate her. She could have easily covered ten miles, maybe more, maybe less."

Jack agreed. "I was also thinking the Comanches probably haven't noticed she's gone, or they would have chased her down and killed her. With luck, they won't notice until they wake in the morning."

"That's when you want to hit them?" Sands asked.

"Even with a full moon, it's too dark to attempt anything before then." Jack surveyed the sky. "Josh, I want you to scout the camp. Take the two Lipans and another man with you."

Sands glanced about him and signaled the two Lipan Apache scouts Nantan and Beasos. Sands' gaze then traveled over the other men in the patrol. Anticipation stood out on Willard Brown's face. Sands pointed to the young man. The three pushed through their companions to Hays' side to listen to the captain reiterate their assignment.

"I'll leave two men with Mrs. Hammer and follow you upstream in two hours," Jack concluded. "Be careful. Their bellies might be full of whiskey, but they're still Comanche. Don't try rescuing the boy until we can attack full strength."

Sands nodded and once more looked at the sleeping woman. Then he walked to the horses. If luck rode with the patrol, by daybreak they might return to Marion Hammer a portion of what her husband's foolishness had robbed from her.

★TWO★

The ride along the creek was like betting a pair when a man knew his opponent held a full house. Sands had no way of determining how far Marion Hammer had run during her escape. Nor did he have a guarantee that with the next bend of the stream they would not be standing in the middle of the Comanche camp. Despite the January cold, a hot, uncomfortable sweat prickled over the ranger.

"How far you reckon we've come?" Willard Brown leaned in his saddle to whisper to Sands.

"Nine, maybe ten miles." Sands held up a hand to halt the three men with him. "I think we should continue on foot from here. Horses make too much noise on these rocks."

Silently, the four dismounted and tied their reins to a stunted oak growing ten feet from the creek. Sands studied the sky. The moon rode near the western horizon; morning was not far away.

"Willard, I want you to remain with the horses." Sands turned to the youth as he once more checked his weapons. "When Jack and the men come, tell them to wait until a half hour before sunrise. If we're not back by then, I doubt we'll be coming back."

He discerned the young man's scowl. Sands understood Willard's disappointment in being left behind, but it did not matter. He could not trust the inexperienced youth if anything should happen when they found the camp. He needed men who knew how to handle a Comanche brave bent on taking a scalp. The Lipan Apaches had fought a blood feud with the Comanche for generations. He did not doubt Nantan's and Beasos' ability. Both had taken scores of jet Comanche manes back to their tribal camp.

Before Willard could voice a protest, Sands led the two Lipan scouts upstream. He looked back once to see Willard, rifle in hand, watching their departure.

The drowsy coat of cotton that had clouded his brain all night suddenly slipped from Sands' mind. His senses came alive. Ears, eyes, even his feet felt a new awareness of his surroundings.

Without consciously focusing his attention, he saw the scrub cedars about him shifting in the rising southerly breeze. His ears filtered the night sounds, separating the rustle of dried leaves from the movement of a jackrabbit that darted through the buffalo grass. His feet sensed the terrain beneath him, placing each step so that he walked as silently as the Indian scouts beside him.

A quarter of a mile from Willard's position, the creek took a ninety degree turn to the east. The high, eroded gully fell away to a rolling rise of rock and earth two feet high.

Sands halted and dropped to his knees, as did the Apaches. Fifty yards ahead stood the wagon. Dark mounds, like elongated ant hills, rose in front of its wheels—the Comanche braves wrapped in their buffalo robes.

The ranger stifled a curse that hung on his tongue. They could proceed no further, and their position lacked a full view of the camp.

Beasos touched Sands' shoulder. The Lipan pointed to the left. A hundred feet beyond the creek bed a hump-like bluff rose thirty feet into the air. Sands smiled and nodded silent approval.

The two scouts dropped back to retrace their steps around the stream's bend with Sands on their heels. Once out of sight of the camp, they climbed the bank and scurried up the backside of the rise. Reaching the top, the three dropped to their bellies.

Sands stared below, taking the camp in with one quick glance. He could not withhold the curse that twisted his thin lips in a low hiss.

The wagon stood in the center of a small valley formed by three sloping rises. Behind the Hammer wagon was a cedar break that ran up the side and covered a long hogback. Acres of the tightly grouped trees darkened the landscape. He did not like it, nor would Jack.

"They sleep." Nantan pointed to the Comanches who lay in a circle about the remnants of a fire. "No guards."

The ranger counted the dark bundles. Marion Hunter had been correct; there were eight braves. Sands could not locate the boy, Jamie.

"At the head of the wagon, near the front wheel," Nantan said with a nod. "The boy."

Sands squinted, barely able to make out the child's blond head poking out beneath a buffalo robe. He had hoped Marion Hunter had been wrong on that count. She was not, which only complicated an already tangled situation.

The brave also beneath that hide blanket had apparently claimed the child as his own, a white son to be raised as a Comanche. Or, perhaps, an item to be sold back to the Texians for a profit.

The thought was unsettling. The Comanches had been quick in learning to exploit the anguish that the captives caused settlers. The more abused a captive appeared, the higher prices whites were willing to pay to have him—or her—returned.

Sands' attention was caught by the horses, still in harness, standing before the wagon. Apparently the braves had been too drunk to unhitch the team, or they intended to drive the wagon and its contents back to their band.

The ranger's gaze roved over the camp again, alighting on sixteen horses staked near the creek. Were the eight extra mounts recently stolen, or were they spare ponies should the braves have to do some hard and fast riding?

Often when pursued, a Comanche would ride one horse until it dropped from exhaustion, then swing onto the back of a pony that he led beside him. A brave could cover a hundred miles in a night by that method, if the situation warranted it.

Sands turned to the Lipans. "Their horses, can you handle them?"

Neither Apache stirred, but stared stone-faced down on the camp. After a few long, silent moments, Nantan looked at the ranger. "We claim ten of the ponies for ourselves."

The Lipans served as scouts and not fighters, and damned well knew it, Sands thought. To endanger themselves beyond the normal risks of their duties, they expected a share of the Comanche loot. Ten mustangs was a high price. Yet, if the Comanche braves ever got to the horses once the attack began, it would be impossible to stop them.

Sands nodded his silent agreement to the terms.

Broad, greedy grins spread across the Lipans' faces. Nantan said, "Tell Captain Hays not to attack until first light. By sunrise, we will be by the ponies."

Without further comment, the scouts crawled backwards. Once off the crest of the hill, they ran in a crouch. Sands watched them swing westward in a wide arc. He lost their dark forms when they dropped into a previously unnoticed gulch.

Satisfied he had seen all there was to see of the camp, Sands scooted from the rise, then made his way back to the creek. With a final glance at the wagon, he started the trot back to Willard's position.

Jack's assurances to Marion Hammer appeared less promising to fulfill by the moment. While Jamie remained with the brave, it would be touch and go. When the patrol attacked, the brave might decide it would be easier to rid himself of his extra baggage with the single slash of a hunting knife across the boy's throat.

Sands tried to convince himself it would be better if the brave escaped with Jamie. The ranger's lies to himself did not help. He had seen what Comanches could do to their captives. That Jamie was but four years old would carry no weight with either Comanche braves or squaws. All that would matter was that the child was white and a *Tejano*.

Sands' pace dropped to an easy walk as he neared Willard and the horses. When he saw their dark silhouettes, he stopped and called out as softly as possible. Willard waved him forward. Sands joined the youth and gave him a quick description of the camp.

"Then Jack was right. We'll have to attack," the young ranger said.

"Either that or let them take the boy." Sands pulled out his tobacco pouch and offered it to Willard.

This time, the young man accepted the bourbon-soaked leaves and stuffed a large wad into his mouth. With a sudden determination, he chewed and spat.

Sands left him alone with his thoughts. Allowing the braves to return to their tipis with Jamie Hammer would not be acceptable to Jack. Willard had been correct, the ranger patrol would attack.

Out of the corner of an eye, Sands studied the young man at his side. It would be Willard's first skirmish with the Comanche, and nothing Sands could say would make it any easier for the youth. A man had to find his own peace with himself and with God when he faced possible death.

Pinching a chaw for himself, Sands squatted beside the creek and waited. The night seemed quieter than it should. Not even the shallow stream murmured. With morning so close, he expected to hear the stirring of birds, the last cries of coyotes returning from their nightly forage. His head lifted and he stared at the sky, watching the slow progress of blue-gray spread across the night's blackness to announce the coming dawn.

The sound of hooves cracking on stone drew him from his thoughts. Jack and the rest of the patrol approached. Signaling Willard to mount, Sands swung astride his black gelding. He was briefing Jack on the situation when Willard joined them.

"If they reach the cedars, we've lost them . . . and the boy," Sands concluded. "Even if the Lipans take their ponies and leave them on foot, I doubt we'd ever find them in that thicket."

Jack sat silent, pondering the information. The captain was not a man Sands would describe as ruthless. If anything John Coffee Hays was one of the gentlest men Sands had ever met.

But when it came to Indians, Hays was the most practical and thorough fighter in the Republic of Texas. Whenever possible, he believed in striking a Comanche camp while it slept.

Ranging was not a matter of sportsmanship, but survival. For each brave killed while wrapped in his buffalo robe, there was one less warrior to fight against the patrol and less possibility of losing a man to a Comanche arrow or bullet.

Sands approved of the policy. It might be brutal and bloody by what some men labeled civilized standards, but Texas was not a civilized nation. It was a rag-tag republic fighting for its life against savages who butchered women and dashed out the brains of infants on wagon wheels.

Jack's tactic might be as barbaric as those of the enemy he fought, but they were effective.

"The way I see it, we hit them quick and clean," Jack finally said. "We'll attack from three sides. I want it done Comanche style, boys, with you screaming your fool lungs out. When they wake, I want them so confused and frightened they won't know which end's their heads and which end's their asses!"

He paused, his gaze falling on Sands. "Josh, you're responsible for the boy. You'll have to take the brave without a gun, but I haven't got a man better with a knife than you."

Sands nodded his acceptance. His right hand moved of its own volition to the blade strapped to his hip.

"The rest of you men stay clear of the brave at the head of the wagon." Jack's voice was firm as he turned to the rest of the men in his command. "I don't want a shot anywhere near that buck. I'll have the hide of the man who accidentally shoots that boy. Understand?"

The rangers nodded and murmured their understanding of the orders. Jack's eyes slowly traveled over his patrol for emphasis.

Sands knew the look, a stare that pierced each man it fell on, as though Jack's words were directed at that individual alone. Perhaps that was the secret of the young captain's success, his power to command men twice his age without any questioning of his ability.

"All right," Jack said. "Follow Josh and fan out quietly when he gives the signal. I'll sound the charge with a single shot. Don't waste ammunition. Hold your shots until they'll do some good."

Jack tilted his head to Sands, who nudged the gelding's flanks and moved forward. The hooves striking an occasional stone, the creaking of saddle leather from the fifteen riders behind him sounded like a full cavalry company to Sands. His steel-blue eyes darted about, expecting to find the Comanches to come whooping down on the patrol, warned by the riotous noise of their movement.

There were no Indians, only the morning's stillness. When the patrol reached the bend in the creek, Sands raised an arm, signaling the men to take their positions.

★THREE★

The rangers divided a hundred yards from the wagon, forming a sweeping semi-circle about the camp. Sands surveyed the formation. In the dusky dimness of predawn, the riders blended with the shadows cast by the gnarled oaks and bushy cedar that dotted the rugged landscape.

Sands sucked a deep breath between his teeth. The waiting started again, the hated waiting. Worse now—action and possible death awaited when the waiting finally ended.

The ranger's gaze swept over the Comanches and their mustangs. He saw no sign of the two Lipan scouts Nantan and Beasos. A niggling doubt ate at his mind. Had they circled the camp as promised, or had they decided to flee?

His eyes rolled up to meet the sky. The eastern horizon now lay tinted with a golden rose hue. The grayness gave way to a pale blue.

Hays nudged his shoulder. Sands turned to find the captain pointing to the camp. One of the braves stirred. Groggily, the Comanche pushed from beneath his buffalo robe and stood.

Sands caught his breath, hoping the brave's mind was still abuzz with last night's whiskey. Halfway to the creek, the warrior stopped. He pushed his breechclout to one side and urinated on the ground. Hours seemed to pass before he drained his bladder. The brave adjusted the breechclout and started to stretch. His head lifted . . . and froze!

A shot exploded beside Sands followed by a howling cry. Sands' heels dug into his mount's sides in answer to Hays' signal shot. The black gelding lunged forward, bearing down on the camp. The screaming yowls of sixteen rangers echoed through the valley.

Two braves came from under their robes at the same instant. A volley of gunfire sounded in a thundering blast.

One of the Comanche jerked rigid, then fell to the ground, face in the dust. The other darted toward the ponies. He covered half the distance to his destination when Nantan stepped from the cedars, raised his rifle and fired. The brave's momentum carried him a yard further before his legs crumpled under him and he joined his companion dead on the ground.

Beasos slid from the cedars and stepped beside his fellow Apache. Together the two Lipans leaped onto the backs of the nearest mustangs. Their arms waved wildly and they shouted to the ponies. The horses bolted, running upstream along the creek. Their task completed, Nantan and Beasos rode after the Comanche stock to claim their reward.

Sands' attention shifted back to the wagon. The other braves were fully awake now. Two coppery-red forms darted into the concealing security of the cedar break. The others scrambled for their weapons to unleash a minor storm of arrows on the charging raiders.

Sands edged the chaotic scene aside, focusing instead on his own mission. His steel-blue eyes searched for the single brave Hays had assigned him.

And he found him—or at least Jamie! The boy sat astride one of the team horses.

Then Sands saw the brave. The Comanche struggled to free a wide-eyed bay from its harness. Trained to the harness or not, the team horse offered the brave an avenue of escape for himself and his captive.

Drawing his hunting knife, Sands spurred his mount on, in an attempt to reach the brave before he realized his efforts were in vain and decided to kill the child and save himself.

Another rider reined a roan into Sands' line of vision. The horse halted beside Jamie. For a dazed moment, Sands' mind refused to register what happened. When it did, it was too late!

The rider was Willard Brown. It appeared to Sands that the young ranger saw an opportunity to rescue Jamie Hammer and had ridden in to snatch him from the back of the bay.

Willard, however, failed to notice the brave struggling to free the horse from its harness. The Comanche *did* see the inexperienced youth.

The warrior grabbed the reins of Willard's roan. The horse reared and Willard Brown tumbled from the saddle to land flat on his back on the rocky ground.

The young man weakly pushed to his elbows, then collapsed to lie motionless. injured or merely dazed, Sands could not be certain, nor was there time to check.

Before Sands could curse the unexpected turn of events, the brave swung atop Willard's roan and pulled Jamie Hammer into the saddle with him. With a yelping, dog-like cry, the Comanche threw himself onto the horse's neck and rode westward in hell for leather desperation.

Shoving his blade back into its sheath, Sands reined the black gelding after the escaping brave and his captive as they disappeared over a low-crested rise.

* * *

The canyon appeared from nowhere. For an hour, Sands had dogged the fleeing brave. Less than a minute before, the Comanche had been in plain sight, riding about a quarter of a mile ahead of the ranger. Then the brave disappeared.

Now Sands understood how the warrior had managed to vanish so abruptly. With a slight tug on the reins, Sands halted his lathered gelding on the edge of the ravine. The ranger easily discerned the moist layer of dirt and sand uncovered by the brave's descent down the sixty degree slope of the wall.

The ranger estimated it was thirty feet to the dry riverbed that formed the floor of the canyon. His gaze rose to peruse the terrain to each side of his position. The ravine ran for a mile to the north and perhaps a half mile to the south.

No matter how he studied the canyon, he did not like what he saw.

The path of the old river twisted and turned. Here and there he could see places where the canyon branched off to the east and west. To ride below would be insane. The ravine offered too many opportunities for the warrior to conceal himself. An ambush would be too easy.

However, Sands had no choice; he had to follow.

Clucking through his teeth to his mount, he moved down the steep slope. The black gelding balked when the sandy soil gave way beneath the weight of its forehooves. By then it was too late. Horse and rider were committed to the descent.

In a half loping walk and half slide, hindlegs tucked to haunches, the horse maneuvered downward. Sand and talus flew into the air around the ranger as he clutched at the saddle horn to maintain his precarious balance while the gelding lurched from side to side. Then with one last bounding leap, the black gelding stood on the canyon floor, nostrils widely aflare and its lathered sides heaving.

Sands leaned forward in the saddle and reassuringly patted the gelding's neck. His gaze moved over the dried riverbed. As hard as sandstone, the canyon floor betrayed no obvious signs the brave had passed this way. Yet, here and there, the ranger detected fresh breaks in the cracked bed. Those breaks led northward.

Easing his rifle from its scabbard, Sands cocked its hammer with his thumb, then nudged the gelding forward.

The ranger's eyes narrowed to slits, constantly moving to take in the canyon before him and the walls to each side. If the brave had an ambush in mind, the attack could come from any direction—even the rear—if the Comanche had time to circle behind his pursuer.

A quarter of a mile in, the ravine narrowed and took a sharp bend to the right. Sands halted the gelding and sat, listening.

The close confines of the canyon walls were perfect for an ambush. Once he started around the bend, there would be no room for turning around. He had to proceed straight ahead, even if he rode into a concealed Comanche camp.

He heard and saw the same thing. Nothing. His finger tightened around the rifle's trigger. Touching the gelding's flanks with his heels, he entered the bend.

The brave waited for him there.

But not in ambush.

Beyond the narrow bend, the canyon yawned wide again, running straight for a hundred yards. Thirty feet from where Sands exited the bend, the warrior stood in the middle of the ravine. Jamie Hammer stood before him, a hunting knife, blade aglint in the sun, at his small throat.

Behind them, Willard Brown's roan limped toward a patch of buffalo grass that sprouted near the base of the canyon wall. Sands watched the abandoned mount shy from placing its full weight on its right foreleg.

With a light tug at the reins, Sands drew his gelding to a complete halt. Ranger and Comanche stood motionless, glaring at one another.

The rifle felt hot and heavy in Sands' hand. Also totally useless. Like it or not, the warrior held the high cards. The brave could draw his blade across the boy's throat before Sands could swing the rifle's stock to his shoulder and squeeze a shot.

The Comanche was apparently very aware of that fact. With a tilt of his head, the warrior indicated that Sands was to throw down his rifle.

Swallowing the curse that tried to push its way through gritted teeth, Sands carefully uncocked the hammer and complied by tossing the rifle aside. He then rode forward and halted ten feet from the Comanche and captive when the brave signaled him to stop.

Again cold steel-blue eyes met equally cold, coal-black Comanche eyes. A hundred possibilities ran through the ranger's mind and were discarded. Even this close he could never move quickly enough to stop the warrior's blade.

For the second time, the brave's head tilted, directing his mounted opponent to abandon the gelding. Again Sands complied.

An uncertain smile moved over the Comanche's lips. Sands sensed the warrior's confidence grow as the brave recognized the ranger's reluctance to bring harm to the child.

The Comanche spoke in his native tongue. The majority of the uttered sounds were alien words lost on the ranger, although Sands understood just enough to feel a ice floe creep up his spine. Playing totally ignorant, he shrugged and shook his head in the hope of buying time.

The ploy was in vain. The brave's gaze honed in on the brace of pistols tucked in Sands' belt, then his head jerked to the side. There was no way Sands could continue his act. The Comanche's gestures were crystal clear.

With two fingers on the handle, Sands drew the pistol on his left side and let it drop to the ground. The brave's gaze moved to the remaining pistol, and he grunted a command that needed no translation; he wanted that last pistol at Sands' feet beside its mate.

And that was the thing Sands couldn't do—not if he wanted to live. Time—he needed time to think, to find an opening. The only way to get that was to delay.

Sucking in a steadying breath and ignoring the beads of sweat prickling across his forehead, Sands used the only delaying ploy left to him. His hand moved again, not to the grip of his pistol, but to the pommel of his hunting knife. He cautiously drew the blade with thumb and forefinger and tossed it toward the warrior.

The Comanche's face darkened, his smile fading. For an instant, the warrior tensed and pressed the keen edge of his blade against the vulnerable softness of Jamie's throat. Sands' pulse raced like a runaway bass drum in anticipation of that flash of steel that would end the boy's life.

It didn't come. Instead the brave once more barked his command and jerked his head at Sands' remaining pistol.

Time had run out; Sands' weapons lay at his feet, except for the single shot pistol still tucked in his belt. If he intended to save Marion Hammer's son and himself, that single shot was his only hope.

Again using thumb and forefinger, Sands slowly eased the pistol from his belt. His arm extended toward the warrior, holding the weapon out as though fully intent on following the Comanche's orders.

In the batting of an eye, Sands' wrist flicked. The pistol nestled smoothly in his palm. His thumb found the hammer and cocked it, as his forefinger curled about the trigger. He swung the barrel up to sight the only portion of the warrior's body that was exposed—his face.

Too late!

The Comanche's reaction was as quick as the ranger's. The brave ducked, using Jamie Hammer as a shield, his knife still at the boy's throat. Once again, he called out for Sands to drop the weapon.

Sands' hand moved from side to side as he searched for a clear shot. There wasn't one. They were at a stand-off. As long as Jamie stood between him and the brave, he couldn't fire; if he took a step forward, the warrior would kill the boy.

Time was on the Comanche's side. Crouched there behind Jamie, the warrior had displayed a cowardly streak, had shamed himself. Sands knew that shame was eating at the brave. Guilt would soon become anger, and anger eventually foolhardy courage. When it did, the hunting knife would flash.

Sands only hope was before that instant, before the brave pulled his blade across the boy's throat, the brave would make a mistake and give him a clean shot.

The exploding bark of black powder rent the canyon's stillness.

Sands' gaze was riveted to the Comanche. His coppery arm jerked outward, hunting knife flying from his twitching fingers. In the next heartbeat, the brave stood, his eyes round and wide and filled with confused disbelief.

Sands' trigger finger tensed then relaxed. There was no

need for his single pistol ball. A dark hole, purple rather than red, neatly opened the brave's left temple.

For an unsteady moment, the warrior swayed as though his body refused to accept the death that had entered his brain. Then he tumbled forward, collapsing face down in the dirt.

Sands stood motionless, uncertain of what had just occurred or why. One instant he had been searching for a clear shot, in the next, his target lay dead. Weak-kneed and hands atremble, he slowly turned to face the sound of hooves coming from behind him.

Willard Brown rode down the steep slope of the canyon, rifle across his saddle. A grin covered his whole face.

"I didn't think he'd ever let the boy go and give me a clear shot." The young man swung down from atop a sorrel mare. "Are you all right, Josh?"

His mind and body felt disjointed and his bladder suddenly ached with bloated pressure, but Sands was all right. Jamie Hammer still lived—as did he! Uncontrollable laughter, a mixture of nervousness and relief, rolled from the ranger's chest and throat.

"Josh?" Willard stared at his companion with disbelief.

"I'm fine." Sands shook his head, reached out and squeezed the youth's shoulder. "How in Hell did you get here?"

"Shorty Green took an arrow in the leg during the attack. When he fell, I grabbed his horse and followed you. If it hadn't been for me, you wouldn't have had to ride after the brave," Willard said. "I saw you enter the canyon and decided to ride the rim."

"Damned lucky for me that you did . . . damned lucky!" Sands glanced around. Jamie Hammer stood twenty feet away staring at them. "Willard, I think it's time we took this boy back to his mother."

Sands stopped and opened his arms. The boy looked at him with uncertainty, then bolted forward, running into the ranger's arms. Sands hugged him close before lifting him atop the sorrel.

"Young man," Sands patted the child's knee, "you'll have the pleasure and honor of riding back with one hell of a man, Willard . . . uh . . . Will Brown. If it weren't for this fine ranger, neither one of us would be going home."

Sands turned to Brown and held out a hand. The younger man accepted the handshake. Sands then looked back up at Jamie. "And I for one am glad he decided to find out what ranging was all about."

The young ranger beamed. When Sands released his hand, he stepped to the mare and mounted behind the boy.

Quickly gathering his scattered weapons, Sands once more swung into the saddle. The ride back would be long, but he did not mind. Did not mind at all.

★FOUR★

"Mommy!" A beaming grin engulfed Jamie Hammer's face as he glanced at Sands and Will Brown. The boy's head swung around, and he excitedly pointed at the camp. "Mommy!"

Sands' perused the camp from the crest of the hogback. Still wearing the loose fitting shirt and breeches the patrol had given her, Marion Hammer moved about the Conestoga wagon below.

"Mommy!" Joy sang in Jamie's voice when it echoed down into the small valley.

"Jamie! Oh my God, Jamie!" Marion Hammer's head jerked up to search and find the source of the beckoning greeting. With arms wide, the woman ran toward the rise . . . and her son.

"Best take the boy down to his Ma. That woman's been through hell. Time she had something good happen." Sands said and watched Will nudge Shorty Green's mare down the hogback.

A moment later mother and child were reunited amid a flurry of tears, hugs, and weepy kisses of joy and love. Nor was Will forgotten as the men gathered about to slap his back and shake his hand.

Sands smiled, savoring a rare moment of self-satisfaction. A portion of Marion Hammer's life was returned to her and life still coursed through his body—courtesy of Will Brown. It was a good day to be alive!

With a cluck of the tongue, Sands eased the black forward. The ranger's gaze traveled over the camp, alighting on two mounds of dirt near the foot of a winter-barren live oak. Wooden crosses rose from the heads of the freshly dug graves.

He didn't need a closer look to know the names that were burned onto the crosses—Felix and Sara Hammer. Two more graves to lie with the hundreds that already existed across the republic. The wind, rain, and sand would topple the crosses within months; buffalo grass would reclaim what man had briefly disturbed. Only names written in a family Bible—and memories of the living—would give testimony that Felix Hammer and his infant daughter had ever lived.

The legacy of a fool, he turned from the graves and looked back at a mother, who clutched a very much alive son.

Sands shook his head. His judgment was tinted with his own bitterness. More than just memories remained of Felix Hammer. A fool he might have been—fool enough to get himself and his baby daughter killed. But he left a son in this world to carry his bloodline into the future.

An unrooted hollowness suffused Sands. Had that Comanche brave had his way in the ravine today, Sands' legacy would have been a money pouch with a few gold pieces, a brace of pistols, a rifle, a worn saddle, a horse, and the clothes on his back.

Who was the bigger fool, Felix Hammer or Joshua Sands? He edged the thought away. He had no wish to ponder the question—or find the answer.

"Josh," Jack Hays' voice boomed from Sands' right and a hand slapped atop his knee. "Damned fine job! I was afraid we'd lost the boy when I saw you take after that buck."

"I'd be meat for the buzzards and ants if it weren't for Will Brown." Sands' head shook, refusing the praise as he dismounted. "You've got the makings of one hell of a ranger there."

Jack glanced at Will in time to see him blush crimson when Marion Hammer delivered a personal "thank you" in the form of a loud kiss to the young man's cheek.

Chuckling at Will's obvious embarrassment, Jack pulled off a wide-brimmed hat and ran a hand through his thick black hair. "I know you'd like a chance to rest up and grab a bite to eat . . . but the day's half spent and I'd like to get the Widow Hammer back to San Antonio before night."

Widow Hammer. Uneasiness ran through Sands. He had thought of Marion Hammer that way himself. Yet to hear it from Jack sounded cold and lifeless. The young redheaded woman was anything but cold and lifeless—and far too young to bear the burden of widowhood.

"Rest on the way back into town," Jack continued. "Hitch your mount to the Hammer wagon. I want you to drive it back."

Sands didn't question the orders, just Hays' definition of rest. Keeping a four-horse team under rein while riding a wagon's unyielding wooden seat wasn't his idea of rest.

As Jack gave the orders to break camp, Sands tied the gelding to the rear of the wagon and helped Marion Hammer and Jamie into the wagon's canvas canopied bed. He then took his place up front. Picking up reins and whip, he kicked off the break and moved out with Hays' signal, stoically resigned to the rough drive back to town.

Fifteen minutes later, the canvas flap behind Sands opened and Marion Hammer's flaming red head poked out. "Jamie's tucked away in some quilts and sound asleep. I thought you'd like some company up here."

Sands smiled and nodded. Reaching back, he pushed the flap wider to allow her to climb forward and settle beside him on the driver's board. Her gaze traveled back to her son for an instant before the flap closed.

"I don't think he realizes what's happened yet . . . that his father and sister are dead." Her head slowly moved from side to side. "Everything happened too fast for his small mind. I'm afraid it'll suddenly catch up with him, and . . ."

Her voice trailed off, and Sands saw the shudder that ran through her body. Her hands clutched in tight balls that left her knuckles glowing white. ". . . catch up with him, and . . ."

"And he'll have you there to comfort him, ma'am. To tell him that in spite of all the bad, everything will work out." It sounded awkward and stiff, the words of a man unaccustomed to comforting others. "He's lucky on that count . . . to have a strong mother there to help."

Sands' memories wove backward through doors he thought had been so carefully locked. His jaw tightened until his teeth ached from the pressure.

For an instant he smelled the smoke and felt the flames that devoured a small supply store on the outskirts of a settlement that now bore the name Austin. He saw his father, skull split by a Comanche war axe. Fingers crept high to the left side of his chest to rub a small scar beneath his buckskin shirt as the pain of a nine-year-old boy, Comanche arrow skewered into his young flesh, re-awoke.

Worse, he heard the screams—the anguished cries of an endless nightmare—that rose above the roar of the flames.

Screams that he would be unable to forget for as long as he lived. The screams of his mother trapped within the blazing inferno.

Sands closed his eyes to force the memories back into their dark recesses, securely burying them—until they crept forth once more to haunt him.

From the corner of an eye he saw Marion Hammer draw a deep breath. Her hands unballed and her gaze rose to the trail ahead. She drew another breath, then turned to him. Reaching out, she rested a soft, warm hand atop one of Sands' weathered hands.

"Thank you, Mister Sands." Her voice trembled and moisture welled in her eyes, but there were no tears. Her face reflected the strength he had seen the night before.

'The name's Josh, ma'am. Mister's what they used to call my Pa." Sands repressed the sudden urge to take Marion Hammer's hand in his own and squeeze it tightly.

She smiled, her hand remaining lightly on his. "My Christian name's Marion. I'd be pleased if you used it."

"Yes, ma'am . . ." Chagrin crept onto Sands' face when he corrected himself. "Marion."

The corners of her mouth lifted in a hint of a smile. For seconds that lingered like hours her hand rested atop his, then she gently withdrew it to leave the glow of her warmth on Sands' skin.

When her gaze turned to the trail, he watched her with stolen glances that left him feeling like some boy in grammar school.

"I guess all that's happened is just catching up with me." The tremble returned to her voice to be quieted with another deep breath. "I can't accept that Felix and Sara are gone. That the plans we made for ourselves and our children mean nothing now . . . yesterday they meant everything."

She hesitated. "To be honest, Josh, I'm not certain what I should do now. I've never been on my own before."

Sands clucked to the team and loosened his hold on the reins as the wagon moved up a grassy hill spotted with mesquite.

Her words came as a statement rather than a plea for help. Another indication of the strength he found within this woman at his side. Had other women he knew survived what Marion had been through, they would be wailing and bemoaning the fate life dealt them. But Sands sensed this diminutive woman's mind working, examining the possibilities that lay before her and trying to judge the best route to take.

Women, hell! Sands eased back on the reins as the team topped the hill. *Most men wouldn't have the presense of mind to do more than sit with their heads in their hands if half their family had just been butchered.*

"There's so much I want to give Jamie. I guess keeping a roof over our heads and food in our stomachs are the first things to worry about," Marion said.

"Reckon food and shelter are all that one needs to get by," Sands answered, recognizing the difficulties that faced a woman alone. "Everything else is icing on the cake. It makes things a mite sweeter, but it ain't needed to enjoy eating good cake."

"Felix left about forty dollars packed away in my cedar chest. That should be enough to get us started. . . ."

Marion shook her head and glanced at the riders ahead of the team. She then looked down at herself. "Guess I don't sound like a widow . . . or even look like one. I don't even own a black dress for mourning. Seems like Felix and Sara deserve that . . . for me to mourn them properly."

With only forty dollars to her name, she couldn't afford to purchase a dress or even the material needed to sew one, Sands realized. Forty dollars could carry a man for a year, maybe two if he didn't mind pinto beans and bacon every meal. For a woman and a child, the amount would only be enough to see them through a few months.

"Do you have any family?" Sands asked.

"My father is in Linnville. That's where Felix and I were coming from," Marion answered, an odd expression on her face.

"Seems to me that's where to start. Families to take care of their own when there's trouble." Sands turned to Marion and smiled. "You can send a letter with someone riding toward the coast."

"Yes." Marion's face brightened. "It shouldn't take more than a month or so to get a letter to my father."

"Meanwhile, if you need money, you've got a wagon and a team that should bring a good price," Sands suggested. "I can handle the sale if you want. But I'd hold on to what you've got until you hear from your Pa."

Marion sat quietly again, and Sands could feel her mind sorting through what he had said in an attempt to piece her life together.

"Mommy!" Jamie cried out over the wagon's rattle and creak. Sands heard tears and fear in the boy's voice. "Mommy! Mommy, where are you?"

Sands barely got the canvas flap open before Marion scurried through, saying in gentle and comforting tones, "It's all right, Jamie. Momma's here. It's all right now."

Before the flap dropped, Sands saw Marion gather her son and nestle him to her breast. His sobs subsided beneath the soothing stroke of her hands and the lullabye she crooned.

Sands smiled as he turned back to the trail. He glanced at the place Marion had sat beside him only seconds ago, uncertain of the loneliness that moved within him.

"Damned fool!" he muttered under his breath as he snaked the whip out to pop it over the team leader's head. He wasn't certain whether he cursed Felix Hammer for leaving a woman like Marion alone—or himself for the unwanted sensations Marion awoke in him.

★FIVE★

A full, angry yellow-orange moon hung low on the eastern horizon when the Hays' patrol rode into San Antonio. Sands sucked at his teeth and silently prayed the *Nermernuh*, the People, the name the Comanches gave themselves, rode far and wide this night. Two long nights had passed without sleep, and two equally long days had gone by with nothing more than hastily chewed bites of stringy jerky to quiet the rumblings of his stomach.

The only thing Sands wanted to attack tonight was a fresh-cut, mesquite-broiled beefsteak. Likewise, the only thing he planned to ride was a sweet dream while he snuggled in a big feather bed with a thick comforter tucked beneath his chin and a fluffy down pillow securely under his head.

Ahead, as he reached the town's main street, Jack Hays signaled his command left toward the garrison.

An amused smile touched Sands' lips. Garrison was a fancy word to describe the long, low-slung, limestone building that served as ranger headquarters. The structure was the solitary reminder of an early Spanish *hacienda* in the area—a bunkhouse once used by *vaqueros*.

While the rest of the patrol followed Jack, Will Brown

reined the mustang he now rode beside the wagon. "Meet you at the *Casa de Chavela?*"

"In about an hour," Sands replied and watched Will ride after the patrol.

Keeping the team on a course down the center of the street, Sands shifted his weight to relieve a backside grown tender from eight hours of spine-jarring bumps and jolts atop an unforgiving hardwood board. Casually he glanced at the dark buildings he passed.

The heart of San Antonio slept. Candles burning within an old Spanish Mission or the occasional harsh glare from a saloon or cantina were the only indications that the town hadn't been abandoned while he had been on patrol.

He had no complaints about the sleepy atmosphere. The quiet meant an absence of trouble. He remembered a Cherokee saying: "The night is for sleeping, or lovemaking." He couldn't recall the rest of that bit of Indian wisdom, but it ended by labeling a man who talked or drank the night away a fool.

On more nights than he wanted to remember, he had made just such a fool of himself. So far the pleasure had been well worth the pain a man always pays for his foolishness.

He by-passed a two-story building with its neighboring saloon, one of San Antonio's two hotels. He did the same to the town's remaining hotel. There was nothing wrong with either of the two establishments. Their rooms were clean, the food good, and the whiskey unwatered.

However, he felt the usual clientele for both was unsuitable for a mother and child alone. Marion had enough troubles now without contending with drifters, gamblers, and local rowdies.

Sands maneuvered the wagon along the dusty, unpaved street to the opposite end of town. There he drew the team to a halt before a large frame house. A single shingle hung above the front porch steps—**Barrett Boarding House.** In smaller letters beneath were painted—**Rooms by the Night or Week.**

Wedging down the brake with the heel of a round-toed boot, Sands smiled at the grand old house with the warm yellow glow of tallow candles coming from its windows. The Widow Barrett had opened her home to boarders three years ago after the money her husband Cranvil had left her ran out. Cran Barrett had served with Sam Houston at San Jacinto the day the Texian army defeated Generalissimo Santa Anna and won Texas' independence. Barrett paid the supreme price for his share of that freedom—his life.

Sands reached behind his back and pushed aside the canvas flap. Marion and Jamie lay nestled together, soundly asleep. He couldn't fathom how either managed to rest with the constant jostling and the deafening rattle of the pans and equipment attached to the wagon's side, but they did, and that was good. Sleep and rest would help heal the wounds the Comanche attack had opened in the souls of woman and boy.

Quickly climbing from the wagon, Sands stretched, and stretched again to work the kinks from his back and legs. He gingerly rubbed his tender backside as he walked up the house's steps. He grimaced; each time he would sit down for the next week, he'd have a painful reminder of the day's drive.

Netty Barrett, her rotund body abustle and a nervous hand patting stray strands of silver hair into place, answered Sands' rap on the door. The woman's bright expression transformed to concern as the ranger recounted all that had happened to his two wards asleep in the wagon.

"I've got food on the stove and beds awaiting," the plump woman said as she directed Sands back to the wagon. "Get that poor woman and child into the house. You tend to getting their things. I'll see to it that they get fed, bathed, and into a clean bed. Now get a move on. A wagon ain't no fit bed for two that's been through what they've suffered!"

"Yes, ma'am!" Sands grinned as he hustled back to the wagon to do exactly as ordered.

Ten minutes later, Sands stood beside a small mountain of trunks and bags piled inside Netty Barrett's door while she directed Jamie toward the kitchen and a fresh apple pie that waited there. Marion Hammer nervously glanced at Sands then shyly looked at the floor.

"I don't know how I'll ever be able to thank you or Captain Hays and all the other rangers for all you've done." She paused as though searching for words that eluded her.

"Ma'am, there's no need." Sands hoped to sidestep an awkward situation.

"I know that everyone of you feel that way, but I don't. I want to thank you . . . for everything." Marion rose on tiptoes and lightly kissed Sands' cheek. She whispered, "My name is Marion, not ma'am, remember?"

Before he could reply, she turned and followed her son into the kitchen. The indefinable hollowness he had felt earlier in the day returned. Forehead furrowed, Sands pondered the strange sensation drawing him to the kitchen door that closed behind the redhead.

"No need to worry yourself about them two," this from Netty, who stared at the ranger. "I'll tend to them."

Sands stepped toward the door, then stopped to dig a hand inside the waist of his buckskin breeches and pull out a small leather pouch. With a tug of its drawstring he opened the sack and shook a single silver coin into Netty's palm.

"She mentioned needing a black dress to properly mourn her husband and daughter. Will you see that she gets one?"

"Be proud to, Mr. Sands," Netty answered and dropped the coin into a pocket of her apron.

With a nod, Sands entered the night. He mounted the wagon, kicked the brake free, and turned the team northward. The horses could be stabled with the patrol's mounts tonight. Tomorrow he'd find someone to pasture the team until Marion decided if she wanted to keep the rig or sell it.

Sands, with knife in one hand and fork in the other, attacked the thick, mesquite-broiled beefsteak. He paused only to spear a boiled potato from the mountain piled on a separate plate on his right or to scoop a steaming portion of pinto beans from the bowl to the left.

Will's attention lay a room away from his meal. His eye wandered to a brunette seated in a corner of the *Casa de Chavela* who was playing the guitar. The most ribald songs Sands had ever heard came from her lips with the sweetness of a woman singing hymns on Sunday morning.

"Sings pretty, doesn't she, Josh?" Will's eyes were riveted to the young woman.

"That she does," Sands managed to say around a mouthful of potato.

He also managed to keep a straight face. The singing first caught Will's attention. What held the young ranger mesmerized was a long, shapely expanse of leg—from ankle to knee—revealed by the brunette's short, ruffled red dress.

"Her name's Adela. She started here last week," Sands said, then gulped down half a cup of steaming coffee.

Laughter broke out at a table to the right, momentarily

drowning Adela's melodious tale of a farmer's daughter and a traveling preacher who freely practiced loving his neighbor. The laughter also drew a scowl from Will.

"What's wrong with them three? Don't they appreciate good music?" the young ranger muttered as his longing gaze returned to Adela—her shapely calves and sweet voice.

Sands shook his head and paused in his beefsteak attack to suggest, "There's an empty table beside her. We could move."

"That wouldn't be right." Will glanced at his fellow ranger. "I wouldn't want to disturb you none."

Sands' attention returned to his meal.

"But, I reckon I can take my plate over yonder." Will stood and crossed the room to settle beside the singer before Sands could utter a reply.

Sands chuckled to himself. Will's plate, one bite gone from the beefsteak, hadn't managed to make the trip across the cantina.

"You have the eating habits of a field hand, Joshua Sands." The voice came from behind the ranger—soft, husky, and very feminine.

"It's only because I feel like a field hand." Sands grinned as he turned to greet the owner of the seductive voice, as well as *Casa de Chavela*.

Elena Chavela, dressed in a black gown of lace and ruffles befitting a Spanish queen, smiled down at Sands. Tortoise shell combs and a single red rose adorned the thick raven black hair piled tight and high atop her head. An open lace fan held in the long, graceful fingers of her right hand fluttered ever so lightly.

The woman's beauty held Sands' eyes beyond the time considered polite and gentlemanly. For the two years he had known Elena, he had been unable to accept that one women could be so beautiful. Elena personified his visions of European princesses his mother had told him about as a child. Surely Elena's Spanish bloodline traced back to those royal houses.

"I noticed your companion's interest and hoped he would be attracted to our little songbird." Elena's eyes, the deep jet of her hair, glinted with impish light. "Adela's bed will be warm this night."

Sands chuckled and shook his head. "I wouldn't wager on that. Will's eyes are bigger than his courage when it comes to women. He'll need time to get over his shyness. He's just a boy."

It was Elena's turn to laugh lightly. "Young, perhaps, but not a boy, Josh. Look at Adela's eyes. That is not the look of a woman admiring a boy."

On second glance, Sands admitted that Elena was right, but he still would have backed his previous statement with silver or gold. Will Brown might be a man, but he still had to convince himself of that fact.

"Joshua Sands, not only do you have the table manners of a field hand," Elena's regal nose wrinkled, "but you have the smell of a field worker!"

A sheepish grin crept across Sands' mouth and he shrugged. "Two days on patrol doesn't leave a man time for soap and water."

"I shall see that it is remedied immediately. I'll have Manuel draw a hot bath." Elena's stare was a stern reprimand. "Be in my rooms in ten minutes."

"Elena, all I want tonight is. . . ."

Sands' words were hushed by a cool finger pressed against his lips and a whisper from the Spanish beauty. "Ten minutes, *mi corazón*."

She turned with a crisp rustle of petticoats and lace. An amused smile plastered on his face, Sands watched Elena float—she did float rather than walk, he decided—across the room to whisper to the bartender. She glanced back at Sands and silently mouthed "ten minutes" before she disappeared down an arched hallway to the left of the cantina's main room.

With a shrug, Sands finished the steak in three bites and corraled the last of the beans with a spoon. Feeling well-fed and sassy, he leaned back in his chair to leisurely sip the last of the coffee.

He stared at the corridor Elena had vanished down. A bath was not part of his twofold plan for the night. The spotless plate before him represented completion of step one. A soft feather bed and hours of undisturbed sleep was the second part of those plans. He had no intention of being sidetracked from his second goal. While he admitted there was a little aroma about him, a bath could—would—wait till morning.

Still he dreaded confronting Elena on that point. The Spanish bloodline that molded her beauty also had given her a truly passionate temper. One Sands avoided religiously. But tonight. . . .

Slowly draining the mug, he drew a deep breath and pushed from the table. Crossing the cantina, he walked down the arched hall. A rap on the heavy, hand-carved wooden door at the end of the corridor brought a bid for him to enter.

Rooms was a correct description of Elena's quarters—five rooms in all. The one Sands entered was a small parlor. It was also empty.

"Elena?" He called out, but received no answer. "Elena?"

"Here, Joshua." Elena's voice came from behind a beaded curtain covering a doorway to the right. "I was just testing the water Manuel prepared."

"Elena . . ." Sands stepped toward the multi-hued strings of glass beads ". . . it's been two nights since I've slept, and. . . ."

Sands swallowed his words when he edged aside the tinkling curtain and poked his head inside the adjoining room. His eyes widened, and he felt his jaw sag in pleasant surprise.

"The water is perfect, Joshua. Nice and hot to ease the aches from stiff muscles." Elena smiled with childlike innocence. Her hair fell long and flowing about her flawless shoulders.

It wasn't her smile Sands focused on. Elena had done a thorough job of testing his bath water. She sat naked within a large wooden tub! The steaming water rippled invitingly about her opulent breasts, playing hide and seek with two nut-brown nipples, that grew firm and erect beneath the caress of his eyes.

A wide grin spread on Sands' face as he peeled his buckskin shirt above his head. Perhaps he had been too hasty in planning the evening. After all, a man needed to be flexible. The olive-skinned beauty who awaited his bath could not be ignored—nor the surging hunger she awoke in his loins.

First a bath, he told himself while he skinned his soiled breeches from his lanky legs, *then the feather bed*.

As for sleep . . . he and Elena could discuss that in a few hours.

★SIX★

Thunder rolled in rumbling fury through Josh Sands' head. He tossed to his side and pulled a pillow over his head. The storm outside might signal a second forty days and nights of rain, but today he didn't intend to get out of bed until he had caught up on too many hours of missed sleep.

The thunder rolled again, sounding closer and hollow.

Hollow? Sands tugged the pillow about his ears. The thunder could sound like a blaring hundred-piece, brass band for all he cared. All he wanted was sleep.

"Sands!" a man's voice called above the next clash of thunder.

Then Elena eased the pillow from his head and whispered, "Joshua, there's someone at the door . . . a man."

Sands flopped on his back, blinking away the blurry veils of sleep. The hollow thunder wasn't thunder at all, but someone beating on the door.

"Sands! Josh Sands!" the voice called again.

"Who is it?" this from Elena.

"It's Captain Jack Hays, ma'am. I'm looking for one of my men . . . Josh Sands."

Sands mouth opened. Elena slapped a hand over it, muffling his words to unintelligible grunts.

"Captain Hays," Elena replied in a cool and indignant way. *"This* is the *home* of a *lady*. There is *no* Josh Sands *here."*

Sands sank down in the bed. San Antonio was free and open as any frontier town. Still a woman had to protect her reputation. One word from him would have soiled the name of the most beautiful and uninhibited woman he had ever had the pleasure to know.

"Yes, ma'am," Jack answered. "I realize that, but one of my men last saw Sands in your cantina last night. I was just . . . I, uh, guess I was mistaken. Sorry to have disturbed you, ma'am."

Sands and Elena listened to Hays' bootsteps retreat down the hall. His captain gone, Sands tossed aside a down comforter and scrambled for his buckskins laying on the floor where he had hastily discarded them the night before.

"A shot of tequila!" he called to Elena as he stepped into his breeches and yanked on his boots.

Elena held a glass of tequila by the time Sands' head poked through the neck of his shirt. He took the glass and upended it, swishing the potent liquor around his mouth before spitting it into a washbasin.

"Appearances, my rose," Sands said, then kissed Elena before grabbing his hat and shoving it down on his head. "Better for the captain to think I was drunk in an alley all night than soiling your virtue. Now back to bed with you—and sleep! I'll be back tonight. Got a feeling whatever Jack has in mind is going to leave me awful dirty."

Naked and all abounce and ajiggle, Elena trotted toward the feather bed. Unable to resist such a delightful temptation, Sands playfully swatted her perky backside. He merely tipped his hat to the string of Spanish curses that came in reply and made a hasty retreat via the backdoor.

In half run down alleys and backways, Sands passed

Jack as he returned to headquarters. For the final touch to his charade, Sands staggered from an alley in front of Hays. He yawned and stretched as though just awakening from a night curled with stray dogs.

"Damn you, Sands! Where the hell have you been!" Jack called out.

"Uh?" Taking a deep breath in preparation for the forthcoming hurricane of profanities, Sands continued his performance with a wobbly turn. "Why, Captain! What are you doing up at this time of the morning?"

The tirade came, passed, and Jack finally got around to what he wanted—three Comanche chiefs had ridden into town at sun up, demanding to see Colonel Henry W. Karnes. Karnes, governor of the region, now delayed the meeting, waiting until Hays could attend the meeting.

"Drunk or not, I want you at the meeting. What little Comanche you speak might come in handy," Jack concluded. "Apparently these three are looking to sign some kind of treaty."

"Treaty?" Sands' surprise was genuine. Comanches had as much need of a treaty as a boar had for teats!

The courthouse looked desolate, out of place. Sands' gaze traveled around the one-room building with its unadorned limestone walls, unable to shake the feeling that the structure had been abandoned by the town.

The desolate feeling stemmed from security measures. Outside two rangers casually leaned beside the courthouses' wooden door, discussing the virtues of Kentucky thoroughbreds versus mustangs. To passers-by on the town's main plaza, they were simply two men arguing incessantly. The two, however, stood guard to make certain no unexpected intrusions interrupted this unscheduled parley.

The inside of the courthouse was barren of all furniture.

Near the door, Colonel Henry Karnes stood, stiff-spined and granite-faced. The Lipan scout Beasos, a former Comanche captive, leaned against the wall. Jack Hays was to Karnes' immediate right, with Sands at his side.

Across the barren room, cross-legged on the packed dirt floor, sat the three Comanche chiefs. Although their arms waved and hands gestured as they spoke, they sat as stiffly as stood their *Tejano* counterparts.

Sands' gaze centered on these three representatives of the *Pehnahterkuh*, the Honey-Eaters, band of the Comanche. The three had donned their finest fringed buckskins and moccasins, decorated with beads and bits of colored glass. None bore the slightest trace of facial hair. While whiskers were a rarity on a red man, neither of the three chiefs even sported eyebrows. Comanche custom required their removal, slowly, painfully, one hair at a time with bone tweezers.

Their hair hung long and shining, slicked with buffalo fat and dung, and adorned with single eagle feathers in the back. At least this was true for two of the three. The oldest was bald with sparse tuffs of white ringing his bare crown. This was Mook-war-ruh, the great *Pehnahterkuh par-riah-boh*, or civil leader. The aged brave's presence added an unexpected gravity to the meeting. Mook-war-ruh was known throughout *Comancheria* and respected even by aloof Antelope-Eaters, the *Kwerharrehnuh* bands.

In spite of the colorful regalia, their obvious tribal markings, the *Pehnahterkuh* appeared estranged and distant from the savage warriors who sprang into Sands' mind at the mere mention of the word Comanche.

For minutes the ranger pondered the strangeness before recognizing its source. *Horses!* The three were unmounted. A Comanche looked incomplete, almost naked when he was on the ground. Astride their mustangs, armed with bows and arrows, war axes, lances, and occasional outmoded rifles, Comanches were the most devastating light cavalry known to modern man.

Short, Sands thought, *and beefy.*

The *Pehnahterkuh* were far shorter and heavier set than the mental image the ranger carried of the fierce warriors. When he watched them enter the courthouse, he sensed an awkwardness in their movements, as though they were out of their element when not seated on the back of mustang ponies.

"This is a waste of time," Jack whispered under his breath as he shifted restlessly. "These three are all *Pehnahterkuh.*"

Sands didn't comment, but Jack was right. The three chiefs were of the *Pehnahterkuh.* The *Kwerharrehnuh, Yampahreekuh, Dertsahnaw-yehkuh,* and *Tahneemuh* were not here, nor had the three chiefs mentioned these other bands.

Chiefs? Sands resisted the urge to shake his head. Chief was a misnomer when applied to the *Nermernuh* as were the terms nation and tribe. Did Colonel Karnes believe dealing with Comanche was like dealing with the Eastern Indians or with the Wacos, Lipans, and Caddoes?

There were no Comanche "tribes." The *Nermernuh* lived in bands that remained together for as long as it suited its members. If a brave was no longer satisfied with a particular band, he simply packed his tipi and joined another.

Nor did a designated "chief" rule these bands. Those whom the band respected were the leaders in times of peace. Their only power was community respect.

As for war chiefs—any brave could gain that title. If he convinced others that his medicine was strong and they should follow him on a raid, then that warrior became a war chief—for that one raiding party. The next day another warrior might gather a party, and he was the war chief of that raid.

Comanches were like no other Indians on the continent. A fact that settlers in the republic seemed unable to grasp. Something that had cost more lives than either whites or Mexicans wanted to be reminded of. Here in the southern frontier region the spilling of blood was the worst.

The three brightly adorned braves abruptly sat silently. They stared across the vacant room, their now mute arms and hands resting in their laps.

Karnes made no immediate response, but leaned to Beasos, whose whispered voice buzzed through the courthouse like the annoying hum of a flying insect.

Sands shifted his weight from one foot to another. He caught just enough of the Lipan's words to be certain the man was giving an accurate translation of what the Comanches proposed. Beasos' inflection echoed Sands' own skepticism.

The whispering stopped, and Colonel Karnes stood straight-backed again. Unflinching, he returned the chiefs' stares across the empty room for several long, silent minutes. He then cleared his throat and began:

"As I understand it, you are offering to treaty with the Republic of Texas, Moor-war-ruh . . ."

Sands gave Karnes a mental nod of approval for correctly pronouncing the old *par-riah-boh's* name. Government officials sometime preferred to create their own names for braves when facing the Comanche tongue. Often the language was too difficult, or a literal translation of a name was offensive to the white ear. The practice of name-changing was used by newspaper reporters who also found Indian names offensive.

Buffalo Pizzle, Wolf's Haunch, and Coyote Droppings were common names among the Comanche. The name

Buffalo Pizzle might stem from a brave's uncanny ability to track bison by smelling where the great shaggy beasts had urinated.

Comanche names were either acquired or bestowed by members of their tribe and usually reflected some medicinal phenomenon or physical attribute with little regard for what whites termed as proper or dignified.

Faced with a name such as Buffalo Urine, journalists refused to provide literal translations in their reports. Instead they substituted a name they felt more dignified and suitable for the sensibilities of their readers.

Sands could only wonder what names journalists would create for these three warriors should reports of this meeting ever reach Jefferson or Washington-On-The-Brazos.

"A treaty between our peoples is an admirable goal," Karnes continued. "One we should strive to attain . . ."

Sands hoped that the Comanches had less trouble believing Karnes than he did. The colonel was a personal friend of Texas President Mirabeau Lamar. Unlike Sam Houston, his predecessor and hero of the war for independence, Lamar believed that every redskin within the Texas borders had to be eradicated like vermin before the land would be safe for settlers.

". . . however, before peace and open trading between our peoples can exist, I reiterate certain provisions that the Comanche must agree to. First . . ."

Sands knew the terms by rote. Time and again they had been placed before the Comanche—with no success. The Texas government wanted the Comanches to recognize the sovereignty of the republic, to leave settlements unmolested, and allow settlers to appropriate lands up to, but short of the plains where the great herds of buffalo grazed each season.

The Mexican and Spanish government before had sought

similar terms. The treaties achieved were at best short-lived. The Comanches weren't a nation, not in the white man's terms. A treaty made with one band did not apply to another.

Did Karnes believe that this would be any different than the treaties that had gone before?

". . . Our main proviso, one that must be met before our people can sit together and talk peace," Karnes said, "is the return of all white captives presently held by the Comanche."

Sands caught his breath. The demand had to be made, but it was one that would not sit well with the three chiefs.

Since 1836 more than two hundred white captives had been carried off by Comanche raiders. Asking the Comanche to return that many women and children, whom the *Nermernuh* considered no more than property, would be the same as asking whites to abruptly release their black slaves.

The three chiefs merely sat silently for a long moment. Then to Sands' surprise, Moor-war-ruh's bald head nodded in what could only be interpreted as agreement. His two companions followed suit. Then the ancient *par-riah-boh* spoke:

"In twenty days we shall return. All the great leaders of the *Pehnahterkuh* will ride at our side. Then we shall continue our talk. Farewell, *Tejanos*."

There was no more to be said. With Moor-war-ruh's words, the Comanches stood and walked out the door. Karnes' mouth sagged visibly, and Sands saw a flush of crimson inflame his whiskered cheeks. The colonel turned to Jack.

"Captain Hays, I want to see you and Sands in my office in an hour from now. I wish to hear your views on what has just transpired."

Karnes pivoted sharply and hastily strode from the courthouse to the plaza outside. Jack glanced at Sands and shook his head.

"I don't need any hour to tell him what I think." Jack started to the door. "We can't base anything on what one band is offering. Any treaty has to be with all the bands, not just the *Pehnahterkuh!*"

Sands nodded in silent agreement. Jack was right. Still, maybe the Comanche were tired of fighting. Perhaps this was a beginning of peace. After all, Mook-war-ruh had nodded his agreement on the demand for return of all the Comanche-held white captives. And there was the fact that Mook-war-ruh himself had come to San Antonio. Why would such a great leader of the *Nermernuh* hold a hand out to whites unless the Comanche wanted something?

Determining what that "something" was, was the job of other men with more authority than Sands. A fact he was glad of. Yet like every Texian, he could hope for the dawn that would bring peace with the Comanche.

★SEVEN★

Sands entered the office behind Jack and closed the door. Colonel Henry Karnes sat at his desk with quill in hand. The only sound in the room was the scratch of inked feather on paper.

"Gentlemen," Karnes began without even a glance at the two rangers, "I have begun a letter to Albert Johnston. Before I detail my recommendations concerning this morning's council to our secretary of war, I would like to have both your opinions of my meeting with those three savages."

The quill stopped. Karnes looked up and he tilted his head to Hays.

The ranger leader pulled his hat from his head and began, "I have no idea what Moor-war-ruh and those other two wanted. I would like to believe that we have finally worn them down. That they're as tired of fighting as we are. However, I just can't believe the Comanches, even if it's only the *Pehnahterkuh*, are willing to call it quits. They've been fighting us too long to just toss down their war lances."

For almost two centuries, Sands thought. The Comanche bands had effectively blocked the western settlement of the continent for nearly two hundred years. The French, the English, the Spanish, and the Mexicans had faced the Comanches and been stopped in every attempt to settle the Great Plains that gave life to the massive herds of buffalo.

The true barbarian, the Comanche was ever at war, if not against whites whose settlements encroached on the borders of *Comancheria*, then on other Indian tribes. Legend held that the Comanche had completely butchered other tribes, wiping them from the face of the earth. Sands could not verify that, but he did know that the Comanche war parties had driven other tribes to the far borders of the republic.

"My sentiments exactly, Captain. My first impulse was to have Moor-war-ruh and his companions arrested when I heard they were here." Karnes nodded with approval of Jack's comments. "I've just written that very thing to Johnston. My hesitance stemmed from the fact that the three were too few to assure our future. Far too many of the murdering savages would have remained free to guarantee the tribe's peaceful conduct. Especially where it concerned hostages they hold."

Karnes paused and his eyes turned to the rough-hewed ceiling of his office. "Also I had to consider the reaction of those in our cities. You realize there is a powerful contingent of merchants who believe we can establish open trade with the Comanche tribes."

"We're Texians, not Comancheros!" Hays' response came sharp and harsh.

Sands felt a deep-seated anger boil up within him at the mention of that single word—*Comancheros*—those hated traders in northern New Mexico who openly dealt with the Comanche. The Comancheros represented an open avenue for firearms and supplies to the Comanches. Guns they turned on Texians.

At the same time, Sands begrudged a slight touch of

The Texians

respect for the settlers of the New Mexico Territory. They, and only they, had ever reached a working peace with the Comanche bands. The New Mexicans had one man to thank for that, the Spanish officer Don Juan Bautista de Anza.

De Anza was a rarity among men on the frontier—one who immediately grasped the nature of the Comanche and understood how to deal with them. Wearied and angered by the relentless attacks of settlements under his jurisdiction, de Anza resolved to fight the mounted *indios* with their own methods.

In the fall of 1779, de Anza brought together a force of lancers, armed civilians, and an army of six hundred, including an auxiliary of more than two hundred fifty Indians from other tribes. When he moved against the Comanche, he moved like the Lords of the Plains themselves. Before his troops traveled wide-ranging Indian scouts, relaying all reports of Comanche movement back to de Anza. The officer then routed his forces via the most devious routes he could find to avoid Comanche detection.

Thus de Anza cut deep into the heart of the eastern Colorado plateau—all the way to the camp of Kuhtsoo-ehkuh, the great war chief the Spaniards called *Cuerno Verde*—Green Horn. The fact Kuhtsoo-ehkuh and his warriors were away raiding did not hinder de Anza. He attacked. Women and children were killed. Lodges were torched. The village was completely destroyed—obliterated.

De Anza then turned back to Santa Fe—or at least rode part of the way back to the city. By a mountain that now bore the name Greenhorn Peak, the officer set his trap—an ambush for the Kuhtsoo-ehkuh and his victorious warriors who returned from a bloody raid on Santa Fe.

When de Anza struck, he gave definition to the word massacre. Kuhtsoo-ehkuh was killed, cut down with the rest of those who rode in his raiding party. The few warriors who escaped were those who fled for their lives when the Spaniards attacked. They carried the tale of the powerful Spaniard back to *Comancheria*.

For four years, de Anza found his hands tied in his campaign against the Comanche—a time Spain was preoccupied with its war against England. But during 1783 and 1784 de Anza once again lead his lancers against the *Nermernuh*. Again de Anza used Comanche tactics against the Indian bands—striking deep into the heart of Comanche territory and butchering isolated bands of Indians wherever he found them.

In 1785, the Comanche rode into New Mexico under a flag of truce, bearing an offer to make peace. It was a peace de Anza refused until he had the promises of all the bands raiding his jurisdiction, which included both *Yampahreekuh* and *Kuhtsoo-ehkuh* Comanche.

The Comanche did not take these promises of peace lightly. They had honored them since 1785. Comanches now rode into Spanish settlements to trade. And New Mexican traders traveled safely on the Comanche plain—allowed into Comanche camps with their goods and their wagons. Thus de Anza had shown a blind world the manner in which to deal with the Lords of the Plains.

And thus had he also created the traders known as Comancheros.

Colonel Karnes' gaze slowly rolled from the ceiling back to Hays. "I did not say that I supported a trade agreement with the Comanche, Captain. I was just ascertaining whether you were aware of the strong support for such an agreement within our republic."

"I'm aware," Hays replied tersely. "I'm also aware that the fools back on the coast are too far from the frontier. They don't remember what a Comanche raiding party can do."

"I'm afraid you're right, Captain." Karnes nodded, then turned to Sands. "And you, Mr. Sands, what did you make of this morning's meeting? Captain Hays had lead me to understand that you speak Comanche."

"Yes, sir. Enough to follow what went on in the courthouse today."

"And your judgment of what transpired?"

"I think Jack . . . uh . . . Captain Hays and I pretty much agree when it comes to the Comanche," Sands said, wishing he weren't within the office.

Dealing with government officials left him uneasy. It was as though they were searching for some way to twist a man's words to their ends no matter what a man meant. Whatever Jack or he said would have little influence on Karnes' final decision. If this were a gaming table he would place his money on the odds that Karnes had reached a decision before Jack and he had entered the office.

Sands continued, "I can't see any harm in listening to what the *Pehnahterkuh* have got to say, but I wouldn't expect much to come from what happened here today. Still if there's a possibility of freeing any of the captives the Comanche have taken over the past four years, it'll be worth our time."

"You have a keen sense of the situation, Mr. Sands." Karnes leaned back in his chair. He extracted a long, black cigar from a box on the desk and lit it, then flipped the lid to the box closed without an offer for the rangers to join him. He blew a thin stream of blue smoke into the air above his head.

"Your summation of the situation is exactly the conclusion I've reached. The republic is outraged by these savage criminals who have raided, raped, and kidnapped our citizens. It is my duty to take all steps necessary to secure the release of captives and return them to their families . . . if at all possible." Karnes drew another deep puff from the cigar. "That is why I'm recommending to the Secretary of War that he appoint a commission to deal with these Moor-war-ruh."

Karnes leaned forward, his elbows planted firmly on his desk. "I'm also recommending that this council be empowered to act decisively, if the situation warrants . . . that troops of the regular Texas army be sent to watch over the council. I'll urge that if the Comanches do not surrender the prisoners as was agreed here today that all Indians who attend the council be seized and held as hostages until all their white captives are released and returned to us.

"I believe the secretary will agree fully with my proposals." Karnes smiled then once more sent a thin stream of smoke into the air. "Captain Hays, Mr. Sands, I want to thank you for your attendance this morning. Your aid and cooperation will be duly noted in my report to the secretary."

Once more the quill rose, and Karnes dipped it into an ink well. The scratching of shaved feather tip on paper began anew.

Jack tilted his head toward the door, signaling the meeting was over. Sands reached out, opened the door and stepped from the office. He released an overly held breath, one that he had not realized he had been holding. It came from his lips as a sigh of sheer relief. Offices and politicians made him nervous.

"I think Karnes has more savvy than I gave him credit for," Hays said as he closed the office door behind them. "The man understands we're dealing with Comanches here and not Tonkawas or Wacos."

Sands nodded, though he was uncertain whether Karnes

understood the situation or was a man who just hated the Comanche. Though the methods used by both types of men were often the same, there was a difference. Captain John Coffee Hays understood the Comanche. And like the Spaniard de Anza, he used the Comanche's own tactic against him. But there was no hatred, just a job that had to be done—and had to be done right.

As for Colonel Henry Karnes? Sands didn't know. Nor did he expect he would ever know. At least as far as Moor-war-ruh and the parley in the courthouse was concerned, Sands doubted that the Comanches would ever return to San Antonio, in spite of their promise to be back in twenty days.

"Jack, if it's all right with you, I'm heading for Netty Barnett's boarding house. I promised Mari . . . Mrs. Hammer I'd help her find a place to graze her stock today." Sands turned to his captain.

"Sure . . ." Jack began, then stopped. "Wait up, Josh. There's something I want to show you first. Something that just might be the edge we need to convince the Comanche to turn their raiding elsewhere."

★EIGHT★

Sands hastily took in the interior of the ranger garrison. Jack's secret edge on the Comanches wasn't meant for his ears alone. The whole patrol was assembled.

Sands looked at Jack with eyebrows arched. "What is this?"

Jack's head tilted to a small man dressed in a black suit and stovepipe hat at the center of the bunkhouse. "This gentleman's got a new pistol. I want him to show ya'll."

"Pistol? I've got two good pistols! What do I need with another pistol?" Sands answered incredulously.

"Ah, sir, I can understand your doubt," the man in black said in a surprisingly deep voice. He lifted a small case from the floor and placed it atop a table next to him. "But this is no ordinary pistol. Captain Hays, would you care to brief your men on this model?"

Jack waved the man off. The ranger then turned to his men. "I *do* want ya'll to listen up. This is important!"

Jack's voice commanded every head in the room to turn back to the man in the black suit. Sands muttered a disgruntled curse. Jack delayed his meeting with Marion for this—a traveling firearms salesman!

"Gentlemen, as I mentioned, this is no ordinary pistol,"

the man in the stovepipe began. His thumbs flicked open the wooden case's flip catches. Opening the lid, he turned the case toward the rangers. "What I have here is revolutionary to the world of personal sidearms—a six-shot revolving pistol."

The red-velvet lined box looked like innumerable pistol cases. The weapon that lay nestled within did not. In fact, the pistol looked like nothing Sands had ever seen before. His skepticism grew as he stared at the pistol.

The salesman lifted the pistol and broke it down into three parts. "Six shots can be loaded into the chambers of this revolving cylinder. I repeat, six shots. The advantage to carrying such a multiple-shot sidearm over single shot weapons is readily apparent. With one simple loading, a man can now carry the equivalent firepower of six pistols."

Sands still wasn't impressed. Stovepipe should try breaking down his pistol on the back of a horse while fleeing a pack of howling Comanches, he thought. He could visualize those parts tumbling from jarred hands and scattering uselessly across the Texas plain.

The history of man's attempts to design a practical multi-shot pistol, or rifle, was as long as the history of firearms. The success was obvious. There simply wasn't any success, or every man on the frontier would be carrying one tucked into his belt.

"What kind of load does she take?" this came from Shorty Greene.

"Thirty-four caliber," the salesman replied while he awkwardly reassembled his revolving pistol.

Sands snorted under his breath. It was too small, too light. A man needed a larger bore weapon when he was ranging. Even a Derringer carried a bigger kick than Stovepipe's pop toy.

"You fire it this simply." Stovepipe eased back the

pistol's hammer with his thumb, pointed the unloaded weapon at the ceiling, and pulled the trigger. The hammer fell with a click upon a empty chamber. Stovepipe smiled out at his captive audience. "We've named this model the 'Texas'."

Sands' attention was on the revolving pistol's trigger mechanism. It was unguarded. That appeared a mite dangerous. Secondly, the trigger disappeared into the body of the pistol when it was squeezed.

"Gentlemen, if you would care to take a closer look at this six-shot revolving pistol, I've arranged some practice targets outside," Stovepipe continued.

No one in the garrison made a move.

"All of you had better take the gentleman up on his offer. I want ya'll to get used to the feel of this pistol. You'll be using them," Jack Hays said. "I've placed an order for each of you. You'll be expected to foot the bill from this month's pay."

"What the hell!" Sands' anger flared at the announcement.

A man accepted to the rangers had to provide his own horse, saddle, pistol, and rifle as it was. But to be ordered to buy a new pistol—one a man wasn't even certain he liked—was going too far.

"Ain't no hell about it. If any man here wants to continue riding with me, he'll be traveling with one of these." Jack's voice tone was firm and cool, signifying he'd take no argument from any of his men. "Those who don't like the idea can pack up and leave right now. I got no use for them."

Sands studied the small Tennesseean's face. There would be no argument, he could see that. He either dug into his pocket and paid the bill or he gathered his belongings and left for . . .

Where? Sands could find no answer. He had no family, no home, no trade. The ranging was all he knew. There was nowhere else to go.

He reluctantly shrugged and turned to Stovepipe. "Guess I'd better take a look at that contraption."

With another wide grin, the salesman lifted the guncase and walked outside the bunkhouse. There he handed Sands the weapon and carefully instructed him on disassembling the pistol and loading its six chambers.

The task was as awkward as it looked. It would be worse on horseback. Although Sands admitted that it wasn't that easy loading his pistols or rifle while astride a running, or even a galloping, horse.

Hefting the weapon in his right hand, he lifted it, pointed at a newspaper target held to the side of a manure pile with rocks, and drew a bead on a small drawing near the center of the paper. His finger curled around the trigger and squeezed.

The report was loud and the kick was what one expected from a small caliber weapon. And, of course, there was the cloud—a minor thunderhead of smoke that always accompanied a black powder explosion.

Sands sidestepped the smoke and glanced at the paper. A smooth round hole lay dead center of the newspaper drawing. Sands nodded to himself, and shifted the revolving pistol to his left hand, and fired once again. When the smoke cleared, the single hole had grown larger by a fraction of an inch.

"Superb marksmanship! Exceptional . . ."

Sands ignored Stovepipe's adulation and turned the pistol over in his hand. It was light and ill-balanced. He examined the manufacturer's name on the side of the pistol and shook his head. Mr. Colt of Paterson, New Jersey had a long way to go before he developed a real pistol a man could use on the range.

Had any man ordered him to buy the pistol except Jack Hays, he would have left that man flat on the ground with a bloody nose. But Hays was Hays, and there was no man Sands respected more, except for maybe Sam Houston.

Handing the pistol to Shorty Greene, Sands dug into his money pouch. He turned to Hays. "How much?"

"Twenty dollars," the captain answered with a hint of a smile.

Sands extracted a single gold coin from the pouch and dropped it into Jack's waiting palm. "You're damned lucky I've got credit at the *Casa de Chavela*. That's the last penny I've got to my name."

"And you're damned lucky I found these pistols," Jack replied with no sympathy in his voice. "Only you don't know it yet. In two weeks when the shipment arrives, you'll see."

Sands grimaced and shook his head.

"Didn't you mention something about finding pasture for Mrs. Hammer's stock?" Jack asked without disguising his disgust at Sands' lack of faith.

Sands nodded and started away as Shorty Green squeezed off a shot. The prospect of spending the afternoon with Marion Hammer was far more appealing than watching men test a weapon they had no interest in—a pistol Sands was certain would make John Coffee Hays look like a jackass to the rest of the ranging companies in the republic.

The team horses tentatively plodded from the barn into the open pasture as though unaware the restraints of man had been removed. Sands watched their heads lift and dark eyes shift as they sized up the situation.

It was a sleek-looking bay mare that first realized the

new found freedom. With a snort and a kick of her heels, she tucked her head low and galloped off. An instant later, the remaining three followed.

"Kind of makes you feel guilty about ever breaking them to harnass, doesn't it?" This from a short, mustached rancher to Marion's left. "They always act like young colts when you set them loose."

Marion, wearing a new black dress, turned to the man. "Mr. Mylius, are you certain I can't pay you something for all the trouble I've put you to?"

"No trouble, ma'am." Sylvester Mylius pushed a sweat and dirt stained hat back on his head. "Those ten acres ain't much more than an overgrown corral. Don't use them except in spring to break a few head of mustangs. Your stock's doing me a favor by eating the winter grass to make way for the spring growth."

Marion shook her head and looked up at Sands who merely shrugged in reply. Her lips pursed thoughtfully when she turned to Mylius again.

"What about storing my wagon? That has to be in your way."

"Nope. That old barn ain't used for nothing much except when I'm breaking mustangs. Don't expect I'd have gone in there all winter if it weren't for ya'll." He paused and glanced down at the ground. "Really, ma'am, you ain't putting me out none."

Apparently Marion noticed the embarrassment that crept into the man's voice, because she backed away from pressing him further. "Mr. Mylius, it's a neighborly and Christian thing you've done for me. Do you by any chance have a favorite pie or cake?"

The rancher's head rose, a smile upturning the corners of his mouth. "I'll admit to a sweet tooth . . . especially when it comes to peach pie and chocolate-cake."

Marion let the matter drop there—an unspoken promise that Sylvester Mylius would get his pie and cake in return for the favor he had performed for the young widow. Sands expected the rancher would receive a steady supply of home-baked desserts, more than adequate pay for some winter grass and use of an old barn.

Mylius glanced toward the sky. " 'Spect ya'll ought to be heading on back to town now. I got my chores and it'll be dark soon."

"Reckon you're right." Sands nodded then stuck out his right hand, shaking Mylius' when the old rancher grasped it. "I'll be out by and by to check on the stock and see if they need anything."

"Be looking for you, Josh." Mylius smiled the smile of a man who realized those visits would also include the delivery of a fresh chocolate cake or peach pie.

Taking Marion's arm, Sands led the young widow to a small buggy he had rented on credit in town. After helping the redhead into the uncovered rig, Sands took his place beside her, lifted the reins, and brought a sleepy old gray to life with a cluck of the tongue.

Sands glanced at the western horizon and the sun that hung low there. He estimated the time at four o'clock. Plenty of time to get Marion back to the boarding house before sundown.

The last thing he needed was the added worry of protecting the reputation of another woman. Elena was enough worry for any man to take on.

"It's a warm day for this late in winter," Marion said as her eyes took in the surrounding countryside of rolling hills brown with winter grass. "Sun feels like a gentle autumn afternoon."

"Almost too warm," Sands answered, leaving unsaid

his hope for a blue norther to drive the Comanche bands to their winter lodges.

"Ohio is probably blanketed in snow by now," Marion said. "And the ponds frozen over. Just perfect for ice skaters."

Sands turned and stared into the smiling face that met him. For a moment the beauty reflected there caused his words to slip away. He awkwardly cleared his throat and looked back to the two wagon ruts that served as a road.

"You hail from Ohio?" he asked abruptly to hide the twinge of embarrassment that suffused him.

"My family had a farm outside Columbus. When I was twelve my father sold it and moved to Texas," she said.

"Illegal immigrants," Sands chuckled. For over a decade before the war of independence the Mexican government had decreed it illegal for any further immigration from the United States. The decree had done little to stop the families who crossed the Red River from the east.

"We had a farm for a couple of years. Then one summer my father broke both his legs when his horse shied from a copperhead and threw him," Marion said. "He lost planting by the time he'd healed, so he went to work for Linn Imports in Linnville. Been working for Mr. Linn ever since."

Marion turned to the ranger. "Does your family hail from Texas."

Sands shook his head. "Tennessee originally. Grandpa came down when Stephen Austin's daddy was out drumming up new settlers for Texas. He settled near Austin."

"They still live there?" Marion asked.

Sands sat silently for a moment, fighting back the rush of tortured memories that attempted to push their way into his head. When he finally spoke, it was softly. "Buried there . . . my family was killed by Comanche."

From the corner of his eye, he saw Marion's face slacken in shock. Her voice was as quiet as his when she spoke. "I guess we both share something that we wish we didn't."

Her hand reached out and took his right to squeeze it gently. "How old were you when it happened?"

"Twelve . . . old enough to fend for myself." Sands shook his head and smiled at the young widow. "I also lie a lot. I wouldn't have made it if it weren't for a grizzly old coot named Billy Byrd. He was with a ranging company that patroled the Fort Parker area. Billy took me in, fed me, saw to it there were clothes on my back, and kept my nose clean. When I was old enough, he took me ranging with him."

"And you've been a ranger ever since?" she asked.

Her hand slid from his, leaving his skin aglow with her warmth. Again Sands felt that uneasiness he had felt that day in the wagon. Also there was the urge to take her hand in his and squeeze it tightly.

He shifted his weight. The rig's padded seat was suddenly rock hard.

"Other than what little farming my Pa taught me, the only thing I know is ranging," Sands said, pausing and pointing to the left. "Mind if I stop and give the gray a drink? There's a creek just over that way a bit."

Marion shook her head, which set the silky redness of her hair flying in the afternoon breeze.

Reining the gray off the road, Sands gave the horse its head and allowed it to follow its nose to the stream. While it drank, he climbed down from the rig and stretched, then rubbed the small of his back.

"You're unaccustomed to driving a wagon, aren't you, Josh?" Marion asked as she stepped from the rig.

"Driven a few, just enough to know what to do and keep myself out of trouble," Sands answered.

"Thought so." Marion nodded at his arms. "My father always says a man's got to keep his back straight when he's working a team, otherwise he'll end up breaking his spine."

Sands smiled. "Expect your daddy's a man who knows what he's talking about. I never set well atop any kind of wagon for long."

Marion moved to his side and turned around. Sands watched her gaze take in their surroundings.

"It's beautiful here in a different sort of way." She looked up at him. "It's a rugged beauty one has to get used to before they can appreciate it."

Rugged was a mild description of the land surrounding San Antonio. It was hill country that grew more rocks and prickly pear than it did grass. The trees were mostly mesquite and bushy cedar. There were a few stunted oaks here and there. And occasionally there were willows that grew near creeks.

It was a harsh land with summers sent up from the bowels of hell and winters that could freeze flesh to the bone.

It was also a good land, a bountiful land a man could live off of, if he knew what he were doing. Besides the rattlesnakes, horned toads, roadrunners, coyote, and buzzards, deer and antelope abounded. There were longhorns, and rabbits, and prairie hens that added variety to the menu.

"It's so different than the coast," Marion continued. "We've got ocean, palm trees and long beaches of snow white sand. It's hard to believe that Linnville and San Antonio are part of the same land."

"It's a big nation. We've got pine forests in the east and desert in the west," Sands said. "Heard one fellar talking in Austin once who said Texas was like a small continent in itself. That any kind of land a man could find in all of North America can be found right here in the republic."

Marion's eyebrows rose. "You don't say."

The gray lifted its head from the creek and turned its attention to a small patch of winter clover.

Sands nodded to the horse and tilted his head to the sun which hung close to the horizon. "Think we'd better be heading back."

"Yes," Marion said and started toward the rig. She stopped and looked back at Sands. "Josh . . . I been thinking about this all day and wasn't certain how to handle it until Mr. Mylius refused my money."

She walked back to Sands, her eyes nervously darting between the ranger and the ground. "Since then I've been pondering on just what to say to you . . . and I guess there isn't any fancy and proper way to say it."

She opened a black string purse on her wrist and reached into it. When her hand came free, she held out a coin.

"Netty told me about this. I thank you for your kindness, but I think Jamie and I have enough to get by on until my father arrives." She pressed the coin into Sands' palm.

"But . . ." Sands stared at her, ". . . the dress . . . Netty?"

"I know what you told her. It was appreciated. But Netty had this dress. She took it in a little for me," Marion explained. "This will more than do. I don't need to go and spend money that isn't mine."

"But . . ." Sands started.

"No 'buts' about it, Joshua Sands," she said firmly. "I appreciate your gracious offer, and the spirit in which it was made, but the need for it has passed."

She leaned forward and lightly kissed his cheek in thank you.

That was the way it started. How it went beyond that point, Sands wasn't sure. But his arms encircled Marion's slim waist, and his lips covered her mouth.

There was a brief instant of resistance, or perhaps it was uncertainty, then she returned his kiss, her arms on his back, pressing herself to him. That was for one heartbeat. In the next, she pulled from his embrace, back-stepped, and glanced to the ground.

"Marion," Sands started.

She shook her head. "I don't know why I allowed that to happen. I didn't mean to. I. . . ."

She stammered, and Sands heard a quavering in her breathing.

"I . . .." she began anew, "I think we should both forget about what just happened."

Sands nodded, then helped her back into the wagon. As he climbed back aboard and took up the reins, he realized that she was right. It would be for the best, if he forgot. After all, what did one kiss mean?

Yet, somehow, he knew he was going to have one hell of a time trying to forget that solitary kiss from the lips of Marion Hammer.

★NINE★

Sands felt naked and vulnerable. In spite of the loaded and powdered long rifle slung securely to his saddle, he felt as though someone were standing at his back with a finger on the trigger of a cocked pistol.

His right hand kept going to his belt to seek the familiar weight of his two pistols. Instead, only the light-weight Colt six-shot, revolving pistol lay tucked there. It provided little comfort.

Stovepipe's two-week delivery date on the sidearms stretched to two and half months before their actual arrival. And today, Captain Jack Hays led a patrol of thirteen men northwest of San Antonio along the Pedernales River carrying the untried weapons.

Two and a half months since we saw these damned things! Sands cursed to himself. In addition to his skepticism of the weapon's ability, he and his companions hadn't been given time to adjust to the pistol. No one had fired more than six rounds with the revolving pistols.

Sands leaned back to rest a hand on his bedroll. Snuggly packed there, he felt the bulges of his old pistols. He smiled without humor. If need be, the Colt could be discarded and the two single-shot pistols could be reached with relative ease. Although the time needed to do even that could cost a man his life.

"You planning to be at the *Casa* tonight?" Will Brown's voice intruded into Sands' thoughts. "Adela promised she'd bake a big cake . . . big enough for the whole company!"

Sands did his best to smile at his companion. Today was Will's eighteenth birthday. The fact that they rode patrol with untried weapons did nothing to reassure Sands that Will would live to see tonight's celebration.

Sands nodded and tried to widen his smile.

"Good." Will beamed. "I was afraid you'd planned to be with the Widow Hammer tonight. You two have been keeping pretty close company the past few months."

"Wouldn't miss the shindig for anything," Sands assured him. "Most of the company'll be there."

Will's grin widened, then his face abruptly sobered. "Are things getting serious between you and Mrs. Hammer?"

Sands raised an eyebrow, as though he wasn't certain what Will meant.

Will shrugged. "Just rumor I reckon. Some of the boys say that you're working up the courage to ask her to marry you."

"Like you said . . . just rumor," Sands answered, feeling a twinge of rootless guilt when he did.

Since that January afternoon, he had been Marion's constant companion. At first he made up excuses that required him to visit Netty's boarding house. The time of pretense had long since passed. He went to the Widow Barrett's for one reason and one reason only. And he had no doubt that Marion knew that reason.

Although there had never been more than that one kiss, Marion never gave any indication she desired the visits to stop. In fact, she had often assured his return with invitations to dine at the boarding house—with the Widow Barrett's approval and watchful eye, of course.

But marriage? The thought was distant and alien to him. He admitted his attraction to Marion. And Jamie Hammer had the makings of a boy who'd grow up to be a fine man. *But marriage?*

Sands had never considered the possibility. While Marion awoke all sorts of strange and undefined sensations within him—things he had never felt with another woman—not even Elena Chavela—he wasn't certain exactly what those feelings were. Nor was he in any rush to put a label on them.

The uneasy thoughts scattered when Jack Hays held up a hand to halt the company. The ranger captain waved Sands to his side and pointed toward the top of the river's bank. The sand there was churned and moist as though cut with a farmer's harrow. However, no farmers lived this far out from San Antonio. Sands nudged the gelding's side to move the black up the shallow bank.

When he reached the broken ground, he swung from his saddle. No harrow, but the hooves of mustangs, heavy with riders, had turned the soil. He glanced to each side. The hoofprints disappeared and the reddish-tan sand lay undisturbed.

As he remounted, he called to Hays, "It was a big party. They passed by here less than an hour ago."

"Comanche?" Hays asked the obvious.

"At least fifty on unshod ponies," Sands replied. "Tracks break off in two directions, moving with the river. Then they disappear. They were trailing brush to wipe out their tracks. Only an accident they left any at all. The bushes probably did a little skip when they hit the top of the bank."

Jack's gaze moved over the rugged, rocky hill country.

His expression said exactly what Sands was thinking—fifty Comanches were too many for a fourteen-man patrol. The object of ranging was to hit the Comanches, do as much damage as possible, then run. In other words, to fight the *Nermernuh* with their own tactics. Head on European confrontation was never designed for fighting mounted Indians—especially not Comanches who were often better horsemen than the whites they faced.

Jack waved a hand southward away from the large band that had passed here so recently. Sands gave his silent approval. The thought of cowardice never entered the ranger's mind. Ranging companies were supposed to kill Comanches—not commit suicide. Fourteen men going against fifty braves would be that—suicide.

Sands reined the gelding up the south bank of the Pedernales and fell into line behind Hays.

Gently rolling hills bordering yawning, unbroken flat lands stretched before the patrol. Here grew thorny mesquite, short, and squat in clumps that resembled overgrown bushes rather than trees. Green sprinkled the semi-barren branches, giving testimony to the early spring that warmed the republic. Unlike the great plains the mesquite here grew freely, unrestrained by white or Indian. Northward, where the buffalo grass sprouted like a luxurious carpet, the Comanches burned the prairie each fall. The devouring flames that seared away the brown grass also burned the mesquite trees that leeched away rich nutrients from the soil.

Here, too, grew cedars and stunted oaks. As with the mesquite, Sands found himself hard-pressed to describe these twisted growths as true trees. He had, after all, seen the forests of East Texas with their towering pines and branching pecans. He had also seen the slender palms of the gulf coast.

The ground bore green traces of early spring grass, but

white, the harsh white of rocks, ranging from pebbles to small boulders pushed up everywhere from the sandy soil. At times Sands wondered why men possessed of their full senses wanted to settle this land when the eastern soil of the United States offered so much.

The answer was simple. As harsh and rugged as it was, Texas was a new land. The game was plentiful, and where water was found, a good life could be built. A good life for a man and a family.

Family?

Sands caught himself. What did he know about a family? He had been raised by rangers since he was twelve years old. His own family was no more than a half-faded memory that often seemed to belong to someone else.

Marion's image floated in his mind. At her side, Jamie smiled up at the ranger.

Had Will's words held a seed of truth? Was the urge to settle down and raise a family finally catching up with Josh Sands?

No. As much as he was attracted to Marion, something was missing. Something he was certain should be there between a man and a woman. While he could not place a finger on what that missing something was, he could feel it, something that was awry and wrong.

"Aieee-ye-ye-ye!"

Sands' head jerked to the right. A cry tore from his throat before he located the source of that blood-curdling scream. "Ambush!"

The warning drowned in a chorus of war cries that rent the air. From both sides, mounted Comanches, their faces painted in the reds and blacks of war, drove their ponies down on the patrol. In one glance, Sands knew he had underestimated the raiding party. At least seventy Comanches howled about him.

Reacting rather than thinking, Sands drove his spurs into the gelding's flanks. An action each ranger did almost simultaneously with his own mount. Fourteen men, as though possessing a single mind, rode southward in a full run.

There was no other course of action. When confronted with a superior force, ranger tactics were simple—ride for cover, any cover, and hold the Comanche off with long rifles. There was no other hope for survival!

Sands heard the sickening thud of an arrow striking solid flesh. Beside him, a man desperately clawed at his back, trying to dislodge the Comanche shaft that jutted there. Then he tumbled from the saddle.

All this Sands saw and comprehended before his mind gave a name to the man at his side—Shorty Green. Sands had shared breakfast with the man that morning. Now . . .

There wasn't time for the dead now. They would be remembered later by survivors who shared a bottle of bourbon and sorrow. If there were any survivors!

Sands' gaze shot around searching for a rock formation, a thick clump of trees. Anything that could be used for cover. There was none. At least nothing close. A half mile away a rocky rise pushed from the ground. The high ground and the boulders atop the ridge might provide the needed cover. Provided the whole patrol wasn't picked off one by one by Comanche arrows before reaching it.

Once again digging his spurs into the gelding's flanks, Sands pushed beside Jack and shouted. "To the right. There's rocks."

Hays turned to his friend, his face set in a deadly grimace. Without a word, he pulled the six-shot pistol free from his belt. His thumb cocked the hammer, and he shook his head.

In the next instant, Jack wheeled his mount. Instead of

retreating from the band, he faced it. The dark barrel of his Colt leveled against the howling horde, he spurred his horse toward the Comanche.

"Crazy bastard!" Sands roared from chest and throat, as he jerked the cylindered pistol from his own belt.

The black, guided by the light touch of leather against its neck, wheeled. Sands reined the horse to Hays' side. No more than three heartbeats passed before the remaining rangers turned their mounts and followed their captain. Fourteen men, one insane captain and thirteen who proved they would follow him into the jaws of Hell itself, raised their Colts and charged into certain death.

The sky darkened.

Sands' eyes lifted but for an instant. A hopeless curse escaped from his lips, "Son of a bitch!"

The first wave of the Comanches' attack descended from a blue, cloudless sky above—arrows! Like a hail storm they fell. Mere bits of cedar, flint, and turkey feather—but oh so deadly.

Sands heard a man scream—another. He had no time to turn for a death count. The warriors, now thrown low against the necks of their ponies were too close—as were the angry-looking war lances they leveled at the charging rangers.

Pain!

Hot and searing, a brand of fire thrust itself into Sands' left forearm. A defiant curse tore from his lips, and his fingers tightened around the reins that sought to slip from his grasp. A Comanche arrow shafted from his arm, its flint head buried deep in his flesh.

Teeth clenched, Sands swiped out with the barrel of the Colt. He sucked in deeply as fresh twinges of pain coursed through his arm when the shaft of the arrow snapped in two. Now he was unencumbered with the awkward length of the shaft.

"Make each shot count!" Hays' voice cried out to his men.

Sands' eyes lifted to meet the howling party of Comanches bowling down on him. His right thumb cocked the hammer of the six-shot revolving pistol from New Jersey while a silent prayer moved between gritted teeth. He sighted a warrior with red and black circles drawn on his cheeks, who rose from the neck of his painted pony with war axe in hand.

Sands never got the chance to fire.

From the corner of his eye, he saw another brave—this one rode down on him from the left. The wicked flint head of his war lance was homed on the gelding's lathered chest.

Ignoring the fiery pain of his forearm, Sands jerked the reins to the right. The black gelding responded immediately, wheeling from the deadly lance that would have skewered its breast.

Sands' right arm swung across his mount's neck. He sighted the Colt dead center of the screaming warrior's face. Knee-to-knee they met. Sands' finger squeezed the trigger.

Lightweight, though it might have been, the report of that mere thirty-four caliber pistol resounded like thunder. The warrior's face was lost in the cloud of smoke that billowed from exploding black powder. His death scream was not.

Not waiting to see if the Comanche tumbled from his pony, Sands returned his attention to the warrior with the circles painted on his cheeks. He found the brave just in time to see Will unleash his Colt point blank into the Comanche's chest. "Cheek Circles" jerked spasmodically, then fell backwards, rolling head over heels across the haunches of his pony.

Around him, Sands heard the barking thunder of "Texas" Colts. A smile touched his lips, only to be erased by a brave who rode at him, long rifle lifting to take aim.

Before the warrior could bring his weapon into play, Sands cocked the hammer of the Colt, felt the trigger once more drop from the pistol's body, pointed rather than sighted, and fired.

The shot was wild—but it did its damage. A dark hole gaped in the coppery-red of the warrior's right shoulder. He cried out in surprise and his rifle fell from his hands as he galloped by the ranger.

Whether that cry was from pain or shock that a pistol that should have been empty was capable of spitting another slug of death, Sands wasn't certain. Nor did he have time to ponder it.

Once more his Colt swung to the right meeting the charge of yet another axe-swinging brave who rode at him out of the clouds of dust. Sands fired. Again his haste cost him accuracy, even at these close quarters. A ribbon of red opened along the brave's neck—a mere flesh wound. The brave grinned certain of victory.

His grin was replaced by sheer horror when Sands fired yet again. The Colt opened a purple hole directly between the warrior's eyes. There was no doubt that this time the horror and shock came from the fact the Comanche was unprepared for a pistol that fired more than one shot.

Then there was only dust. As quickly as it had begun, it was over. He had ridden through the full charge of seventy Comanche warriors and lived! He was alive!

Sands' head jerked from side to side. He saw Will grinning, smoke still trailing from the barrel of his Colt.

And there was Hays and Wallace . . . and Utley and . . . at least ten of the patrol still lived.

Sands wheeled the gelding about. On the ground were a dozen braves—the bloody proof of the Colt's value and Jack Hays' ability as a leader.

Beyond the settling dust, the diminished war party of painted warriors sat on their ponies, staring in disbelief at the havoc wrecked by such a small band of white men.

"Empty your pistols! Then take 'em with your rifles!" The cry came from Jack Hays.

Sands responded immediately. He leveled his Colt, took aim and squeezed off his fifth shot. A lance-bearing brave slumped across the neck of his pony, then slid to the ground.

Before Sands could fire the remaining shot in his Colt's cylinder, five other warriors fell victim to the blazing six-shot revolving pistols that were so deadly in the rangers' hands.

The remaining shot in the Colt was wasted. The brave Sands sighted on wheeled his mount wildly, just as the ranger squeezed the disappearing trigger.

In the next instant, the whole party was doing the same. Jerking the heads of their mounts around, they fled!

Sands reached for his rifle, suddenly very much aware of the limitations of that one-shot weapon.

"Son of a bitch!" Unrestrained the curse roared from Sands' snarled lips as Will grasped the broken arrow shaft and yanked the embedded head free.

A string of curses that would have made a sailor blush followed as the young ranger washed the wound with water from his canteen, then poured a healthy shot of medicinal bourbon into the open wound.

Sands' curses dwindled to a mutter by the time Will

wrapped the arm with a strip of bandage pulled from a saddlebag.

"With all that venom in you, it's a surprise you lived this long!" Will laughed as he tied off the bandage. "Never heard a man complain so much about a little scratch before!"

"Little scratch! Why you son-of-a-whore, I'll put a scratch up side your head . . ."

Sands were cut short by a chorus of rifle fire. A shiver went through him. The last victims of today's melee fell somewhere beyond the rise to the north. These were not men, but ten Comanche ponies taken during the fighting. As much as it pained any man who appreciated good horse flesh, the Indians' horses were killed whenever possible. The fact was simple, a Comanche brave on foot posed little danger—on horseback he was a killer.

"Here, I reloaded for you." Will handed Sands his pistol.

Tucking the weapon into his belt, Sands stood and walked to the gelding that stood tied to a barren oak. He mounted, as did Will. "Best we rejoin the others. It's a long way back to your party tonight."

Will smiled and nodded. The youthful enthusiasm that had been there this morning was missing now. The young ranger's expression was one of relief at still being alive. Something that four of their patrol could not share.

Sands' fingertips touched the pistol at his waist. He had been wrong about the six-shot revolving pistol, he now realized. Hays had been right. Were it not for Mr. Colt's pistol and Captain Jack Hays the whole patrol would have been killed today. But then that's why Jack was a captain and he was just a ranger.

Instead of fifteen massacred men laying in the sand, thirty Comanches had died. Thirty warriors out of a war party of seventy! It was unheard of! Then, too, so was this marvelous weapon that had come to the frontier today.

As Sands rode up the rise to rejoin the rest of the patrol, he remembered the two pistols tucked into his sleeping roll. He wondered if he could find a buyer for the weapons before news of Colt's revolving pistol got out.

★ TEN ★

Thirty rangers crowded into the *Casa de Chavela* to raise their voices in unabandoned celebration—a roar that equaled at least sixty ordinary men. The amount of whiskey—the good bourbon had long been replaced by red-eye—and tequila consumed equalled at least ninety.

Sands watched while he sat in a corner isolated from the boisterous mass of rangers who groped for each of Elena's passing girls. Will's birthday provided the excuse for the revelry, but there was more, something that loud voices and bawdy jokes could not disguise. Nor could it be drowned in alcohol.

Tonight the rangers shared a rite that had been observed by soldiers and warriors through the ages. They celebrated victory and the life that still coursed through their veins. In doing so, they honored the four who had fallen beneath the Comanche arrows today.

Whether his fellow rangers or the republic recognized the fact, they *were* soldiers. Soldiers in a long and bloody war that had no end in sight.

Unless. For a moment his thoughts returned to Moor-war-ruh and the two chiefs who had ridden into San Antonio. They had promised to return in twenty days.

Sands sucked at his teeth. That had been more than two and a half months ago. To believe the Comanche wanted peace was a fool's game. Since the meeting with Colonel Karnes, the *Nermernuh* raiding parties had continued without the slightest sign of slackening. If Moor-war-ruh ever returned to San Antonio, it would be at the head of a war party.

"It seems your friend Will is about to receive Adela's birthday present." Cool feminine fingers rested on the back of Sands' neck, playing with the shaggy brown hair resting there.

Sands looked up into Elena Chavela's smiling face. Her raven black eyes motioned Sands' gaze across the room.

There Will and the young singer, eyes longingly locked on one another, quietly walked arm-in-arm from the cantina's main room toward Adela's room in the back.

"I'm glad I did not wager with you that first night Will came into my cantina," Elena said with a shrug. "He is a shy boy when it comes to women. For two months Adela has been trying to get him to her room."

"He won't be a boy after tonight." Sands chuckled. "I think Adela will find it'll be a damn sight harder task to keep him out of her room than it was getting him in it."

Elena smiled, her fingers continued their playful taunting. "Speaking of rooms. I will be going to mine shortly. Manuel has already drawn a hot bath for me."

With another smile and a light squeeze of his neck, she moved on to another table. Sands had no doubt that the waiting bath was an invitation for him to discreetly join her when the opportunity arose.

Lifting his glass, he took a bite from a wedge of lemon, licked the salt on the back of his hand, and slugged down a healthy portion of his glass of tequila. He watched Elena, like some regal princess, make a round of the cantina, laughing and welcoming the rangers. The circuit completed, she smiled over her shoulder at Sands before disappearing down the arched corridor that led to her chambers.

Sands downed the remainder of the tequila and stood. A man couldn't ask for more than to have a woman like Elena waiting when he returned from patrol. Nor could he ask for more comfort than he found in Elena's feather bed.

Which is why Sands couldn't understand what made him walk from the cantina and ride toward Barrett's Boarding House.

"You're wounded!" Marion's emerald green eyes held genuine concern when she greeted him at the door.

Before Sands could explain, she led him into the parlor, with Jamie and Netty Barrett following at her heels, and demanded that he sit quietly while she cleaned and redressed the wound.

While his mother gently labored, Jamie craned over her shoulder to get an unobstructed view of the wound and plied Sands with a thousand and one questions about the day's melee. The boy listened attentively, reveling in the grisly details of the battle with relish. It was a good sign. In spite of everything the youngster had suffered at the hands of the Comanches, he bore no scars—or at least the ones he had were healing.

"It's past your bedtime, young man," Marion said when she completed rebandaging the wound. Marion looked at Netty. "Will you see that he bathes and gets to bed?"

The older woman nodded and tugged a balking and loudly protesting Jamie from the parlor. Marion looked back at Sands with brow knitted and concern still in her gem-green eyes.

Sands shook his head. "It's over now. Other than some soreness, I'm no worse for the wear."

Marion's lips parted. They trembled, but no sound passed them. Then she bit at her lower lip, and her eyes rolled to the waxed hardwood floor. Her head, its red strands neatly tucked into a loose bun, moved slowly from side to side.

Sands could only guess at what weaved through her mind. Her own encounter with the Comanche, the murder of her infant daughter and husband were all still too close. Sands tried to find the words to reassure her. Nothing seemed appropriate. Words had always come hard to him, especially with women.

"I was hoping we could take a walk down by the river," Sands said, aware of the awkward sound of his own voice. "The night's warm and there's a sliver of a moon in the sky."

The smile on Marion's lips barely uplifted the corners of her mouth when her eyes rolled up, but she nodded.

Grabbing his hat from the sofa, Sands stood and offered Marion his arm. She accepted it after she scurried to her room to retrieve a shawl and tell Netty of their walk.

"I got a raised eyebrow from Netty, but no motherly warning about protecting my honor," Marion said as they walked out the house's rear door and carefully picked their way through Netty's garden. "She's like my mother in a lot of ways . . . some of her attitudes. An unmarried woman shouldn't be out after sunset with a man unless she's accompanied by an escort."

Marion laughed as they reached the bank of the San Antonio River and began walking southward along a narrow, foot-worn path. "But she says you're a good man . . . a few rough edges . . . but trustworthy and honorable."

"Rough edges?" Sands said in mock dismay. "I kick the mud from my boots and take off my hat when I enter a house."

"You also smoke, chew, and drink. All deadly sins to

Netty. Then, too, there are rumors of the hearts broken by a handsome, young ranger named Joshua Sands." Marion paused beside a budding willow.

Sands said nothing. He wasn't certain what she meant by the "broken hearts" comment, what she delved for from him, but no man in his right mind would ever touch a remark like that.

He looked out over the San Antonio river. It ran like a black band of velvet lazily cutting through the land. While less than a hundred feet wide, small by comparison to the great rivers of the East like the Mississippi, and the Ohio, in a land where water was often as precious as rare metals, it held a beauty all its own. Tonight, the waning moon that hung overhead lit the ripples of its surface like a myriad of twinkling diamonds.

"We're only a short walk from the house and it seems like we could be miles from town," Marion whispered in an almost reverent voice.

She was right. Here they were beyond the lights of the town. Beyond the town itself. The night held a stillness Sands had only found when he was ranging.

"Mind if we just sit and look at the river rather than walking further?" Marion asked, lowering herself beside the willow when Sands nodded.

"I also think Netty is tolerant because she realizes how much I need the company of someone right now." Marion turned to Sands, her face softly lit in the misty moonlight. "I don't know what I would have done without having you here to help."

"Don't underestimate yourself." Sands shook his head. "You've got more steel in your spine than half the men I've met."

"No, you're wrong, Josh. I'm stubborn, but I've never been strong." Her voice went soft again, distant. "That's why I nearly broke down tonight when I saw your arm. Like it or not, Josh, I've grown to depend on seeing your face and hearing your voice. Sometimes, I think your strength is the only thing that kept me from going insane those first few weeks . . ."

She paused and drew a long breath. "Tonight when I saw your arm and heard everything you told Jamie, I realized that you might have been killed. I couldn't take that, Josh. I couldn't endure having another person I care about being taken from me. I . . . not now . . . I couldn't . . ."

For the first time since the night the raiding party had killed her husband and daughter, Sands saw tears well from Marion's eyes and trickle down the beauty of her cheeks. Something deep within his chest twisted and tore. His arms reached out and encircled the small woman, easing her to him.

"Shhhh," he whispered. "It's over now. I'm all right. In a week or two, you won't even be able to tell which arm got hit. It's all over."

"You . . . you could have been one of the four you buried this afternoon." Marion's head lifted, her eyes meeting his. "Don't you understand . . . I care for you, Josh. I . . ."

His mouth covered hers muffling that single word that he knew was forming on her lips. A word he realized he had yearned to hear from this small, redheaded woman since that day he had driven her wagon into San Antonio.

Yet one he could not bear the hearing.

Love. It echoed in his mind. He ached to hear it from Marion, but could not. Something dark slithered within his chest, something that avoided definition, that prevented his tongue from forming that single word. He had whispered that word in the ears of more young women and *señoritas* than he could remember in order to pave the way to their beds. But now, with this woman who made him feel as though his veins ran warm with wine, who evoked all the things a woman was supposed to fire within a man, he could not say—*I love you*. Nor could he understand his hesitance.

He did understand the lips pressed warmly to his. Their hunger held a rightness that seemed natural. He shared that hunger—that of a man for a woman, a woman for a man. A desire he had held tightly in rein since the evening they had returned from Mylius' ranch.

Together, locked in their embrace, they eased back, atop a bed of spring grass. She questioned with neither voice nor expression when his fingers moved to the tangled myriad of buttons and clasps securely binding her dress. She did shift beneath the guiding pressure of his palms, allowing him to free each of the encumbering obstacles.

Her hands found the wooden buttons to his flannel shirt and easily worked them free. Her fingers and the softness of her warm lips explored the broad expanse of his chest, by the time he slipped the last of her feminine underclothing from her body.

Mist-like in the soft moonlight, she lay beside him. Her eyes rose to his. There was no hint of shame in the gentle radiance of her face. No trace of hesitance. Only the rightness that Sands had sensed before.

His eyes, followed by the feathery touch of his fingertips, traced over the graceful length of her neck downward to the twin mounds of her breasts. A sudden gasp of pleasure escaped her lips as his palms cupped those delightfully uplifted cones. His fingers molded warm, pliant flesh, while his thumbs busied the coral-hued buds atop each, bringing them to aroused attention.

Then his head lowered, and his lips and flicking tongue

joined his taunting fingertips. She answered his attentiveness with a soft, throaty coo of satisfaction.

Sands lost himself in the luxurious feel of her, the satiny texture of her body that shifted and turned to accommodate the intimate exploring of his seeking fingertips. There were no whispered promises, no lies to justify their act. His hands spoke and hers answered.

Even the awkwardness that came when caresses were broken for Sands to remove his remaining clothing, seemed but one pounding heartbeat. Then he lay at her side, flesh touching flesh, no longer restrained by the coarse weave of fabric.

She opened her arms, and he came to her, entering the liquid heat of her body in one flowing motion. In a slow sleepy rhythm, they rocked together while their hands and fingers touched, caressed, soothed, and tautened.

Together—always together—they found and fed their needs. Their desire flamed to devouring passion that ended as her body suddenly went rigid and her hands dug into the rock-hard balls of his buttocks.

Sands' mouth once again covered hers, muffling her uninhibited cries of pleasure released, as the fire within his own core erupted to flow forth.

Together, man and woman, they lay locked into each other's arms, savoring the sensations of one another, neither wishing to break this most intimate of bonds they had forged beneath the starry sky.

★ELEVEN★

The most satisfied man on God's green earth—a man who won and shared the love of a magnificent woman—that was the way it should have been for Sands.

Instead, something was amiss. A dark seed, one beyond his comprehension, sprouted amid the gentle warmth Marion awoke within him. Sands muttered a curse, unable to find the root of his dissatisfaction.

He was a fool. Marion offered everything that a man could ever want—all he envisioned for his own life. With her, he could rebuild the family the Comanches had stolen from him.

In that moment, he realized that a family was what he wanted from life. When he was twelve-years-old, Josh Sands witnessed his family butchered by a savage raiding party. Since that time he had searched to find someone—something—to replace what had been brutally torn from him.

Like his old mentor Billy Byrd, he thought that he had filled his emptiness with ranging. But Marion and Jamie threw light into the vacant rooms of his life, illuminating his true loneliness.

With them he could erase that loneliness. Yet he could

not accept what they offered. Something, that elusive something, between Marion and him was wrong.

The rightness he felt while he lay with Marion beside the San Antonio River flooded back into his mind. Even Elena with her totally uninhibited lovemaking could not equal what he had found this night.

The dark seed of doubt bloomed. Its black petals spread wide to smother the tenderness of that moment.

"Damned fool!" he spat as he rode through San Antonio's streets.

He didn't want to think: he wanted to escape the darkness gnawing in his chest. There was only one certain way to do that—bourbon—and lots of it.

Ahead, he heard the revelry still coming from the *Casa de Chavela*. Ordinarily, he would have rejoined his companions to lose himself in the celebration.

Tonight, he reined the black gelding to the opposite side of the street and by-passed the cantina. He felt like some alley dog cowering away with its tail tucked between its legs, but he couldn't face Elena again tonight. Not because he had slipped out and left her alone in the waiting bath tub. Elena would only remind him of Marion—that was the very thing he wanted to escape.

Nudging the gelding into a easy lope, he moved down the street and stopped before the *Longhorn Saloon*. With a hastily looped slip-knot, he hitched the horse to a cedar rail outside, then entered the saloon through the swinging doors. Here and there a few men looked up from where they sat huddled about the round tables, but the majority of the *Longhorn*'s patrons didn't notice his entry. Which suited Sands; it wasn't companionship he wanted. He walked to the bar and ordered a bottle of bourbon and a glass. When the bartender brought his order, he quickly poured two fingers and downed it.

The whiskey was cheap, raw, and tasted like it had been aged a month before bottling. He didn't care. Taste wasn't what he was after. He poured another slug and downed it without blinking. Three drinks, maybe five, and he would be well on the way to forgetting Marion. Then he'd take the bottle, return to the garrison, and quietly drink himself into oblivion. Tomorrow, maybe the day after, he'd get things sorted. Right now everything was too close, pressing.

Sands once more lifted the bottle and poured a stout measure of the amber liquor into his glass. This he sipped rather than downing on one gulp. After all, he wanted to get drunk, not sick.

"Josh . . . Josh Sands is the name, ain't it?" A barrel-chested man moved from the opposite side of the bar to Sands' side in a watery walk that spoke of many hours of hard drinking.

Sands gave him a casual glance. The man's black stubble beard, that appeared to be a two-week unshaven growth rather than a cultivated beard, looked familiar, but Sands couldn't put a name with the face hidden behind the untidy whiskers. So he merely nodded and took another sip from his glass.

"Ellis, Ellis Thompson out of Corpus Christi." The man held out a bear-sized paw. "We met last time I rode courier . . . about three months back."

No smile touched Sands lips as he recalled the loud-mouthed ranger out of Corpus Christi. Three months ago, the man had ridden down with a communique for Colonel Karnes. Before he rode back south the following morning, he had drunk enough tequila to float a small navy, then had gotten into a fight with three local ranch hands. The results were one broken jaw, a fractured arm, and three broken ribs—none of which Thompson suffered.

"Riding courier again?" Sands asked without caring.

Three more sips and he'd be through with the drink and on his way to the garrison, free of Thompson's company.

"Town's quiet. I was hoping for a little more activity." The Corpus Christi ranger punctuated his remark with a wink.

Sands started to tell him about the shindig at the *Casa*, paused, then realized the men in Hays' company were capable of handling someone like Thompson if need be, and told the ranger about the celebration down the street.

Thompson shook his head. "Ain't got no use for greasy pepper-bellies. Never cared for dark meat. White is sweeter."

Sands' hand tightened around his glass, but he said nothing, just let another sip of the raw bourbon roll down his throat.

"But then, I forget this is San Antonio," Thompson said, his eyes narrowing as he stared at Sands. "It's well-known that the men in the Hays company ain't particular whose bed they sleep in."

"Seems that's a man's own business and no concern to anyone else." Sands repressed the anger stirring within him. Thompson was apparently liquor-mean and itching to fight. And not that particular who he took on. Had he been a drifter or a ranch hand, Sands would have obliged him. But the man was another ranger—even though he hailed from Corpus Christi. Common courtesy required greater tolerance of his condition.

"I'd expect something like that from you." Thompson replied, viciousness creeping into his voice as it grew louder with each word.

Sands lowered his glass and slowly turned to Thompson, one eyebrow arching high. He felt heads turning toward him as the saloon's patrons sensed a fight in the air. For a moment, he almost forgot this bear-of-a-man was a ranger and pressed for an explanation of his comment. Instead, Sands raised the glass to drain the last of the bourbon.

"I hear you've found yourself a cosy little piece to warm the nights," Thompson continued, his tone and face a mocking sneer.

Sands shoved the cork back into the mouth of the bottle. "It's been a long day, Ellis. As much as I've enjoyed the company, I'm long overdue a good night's sleep."

"Ha! Ain't no sleep you're after, Sands." The laugh that came from Thompson's throat was obscene. "My bet's you're off to see that widow lady. The one I heard you got secreted off on the other side of town. Every man in your company's talking about what you got going on the side."

Sands stiffened and caught himself before he slammed the bourbon bottle into Thompson's face. As much as the man deserved it, a shattered bottle would be a waste, even of cheap whiskey. Sands stepped toward the door of the saloon. "Thompson, you've had too much to drink, and I'm tired. If you want to continue this in the morning, I'll be glad . . ."

"How many Comanches had her, Sands? Ten? Twenty?" Thompson grinned wickedly, his dark eyes afire. "She's tainted now, Sands. Rather pay my two-bits and take my chances with a whore than have a woman like that. No respectable man would touch a white woman after she's been used by red scum. No man would . . ."

"I thought you were talking about yourself, Thompson. No respectable man would mention a lady while in a saloon. Then no one ever said anything about you being respectable. And you can be damned sure no one's ever mistaken you for a man," Sands said, with his back still to the barrel-chested ranger.

He felt the black blossom within his chest spread its

petals wider as he carefully deposited the bourbon on the bar. Fury boiled at his core. He turned on the balls of his feet. That was the sole warning he gave to the right he threw in Thompson's face.

"Ooumph!" Surprise and shock flew from the bear-sized ranger's mouth as Sands punch landed squarely atop a bulbous nose.

Sands felt and heard the cartilage and bone give way beneath his fist. He watched Thompson stagger back, eyes wide and mouth agape. A normal man would have gone down under such a solid blow. The excruciating pain of a broken nose usually left a man totally disoriented and vomiting out his guts. Thompson merely staggered.

Sands didn't wait for the loud-mouthed ranger to recover from that stagger. Taking two quick steps forward, Sands sunk a hard left into the man's gut and followed it with a right to the same spot.

The blows were wasted. While Thompson's stomach equalled his chest in size, it was also rock hard with muscles firm and strong.

Roaring in alcohol-hazed anger and pain, Thompson's arms stretched wide, seeking to ensnare his smaller-built opponent. His arms closed around empty air.

Sands simply ducked and lunged to the right to avoid the man's bear hug. As he did, he sent the rounded toe of a boot flying upward to bury itself in Thompson's crotch.

The over-grown ranger did more than stagger now. He howled in agony. Grasping that most vulnerable portion of his body, he doubled over.

Which was exactly what Sands wanted. His own knee jerked up and slammed into Thompson's face. When the man's head reeled back from the impact, Sands added a hard swung right to the chin.

For one indecisive moment, Thompson swayed, his eyes

blinked with uncertainty. Then those eyes closed and he toppled backwards like some tall oak felled by a razor-honed ax. He hit the pine floor of the saloon solidly and lay there unconscious to the room full of men who stared down at his defeat.

Straightening the brim of his hat, Sands turned, snatched his bottle from the bar, and walked from the *Longhorn*. As much as Thompson had deserved what he had gotten, Sands discovered he held no anger for the ranger. The fury that still screamed like a gulf hurricane within him was not for Thompson, but for himself.

Thompson's words had contained more than a seed of truth. Naked and ugly, the man had opened Sands' eyes to himself. What he saw was something dark and dirty. And that something was Marion Hammer. In spite of all that he felt for her, all she had given him, he could not accept her as she was—as a woman who had been used by Comanche.

Sands swung astride the gelding and yanked the cork from the neck of the bottle. Without tasting the whiskey, he sucked three large swallows down his throat.

That was the hell of it! Deep inside him, deep at the core of his being, he and Thompson were no different. And neither of them were worth Marion's spit!

He jerked the gelding's head around with a viciousness intended for himself rather than the black and dug his heels into the horse's side. With a snort the gelding bolted forward in a dead run.

Sands lifted the bottle to his lips. He hesitated, staring at the amber liquid that sloshed about inside. With all the self-directed hate that stormed within him, he slung the bottle aside. He heard a window shatter, but didn't look back. Tomorrow, he would seek out a merchant and pay for the damages. Tonight he needed to ride, to get away from San Antonio and the spider's web he had spun for himself.

The same sliver of moon that had bathed the perfection of Marion's body now hung low on the western horizon as Sands rode silently back toward San Antonio. The hours alone had done nothing to resolve or erase the ugliness he had found within himself.

Love—the simple word he had been unable to utter—was real. He did love Marion. No other woman had ever touched him the way the young widow did. Yet he could not remove the vision of eight Comanches taking her body—the same body she so willingly gave to him. That she had been raped, forced to submit to their lusts, did not matter. Thompson's words kept echoing in his head—*tainted—tainted—tainted*.

The easiest course to take was to turn his back on the woman—to walk away from her. That he could never do. He yearned to possess her and all that she offered. He knew he would see her again, although he was uncertain how he could face the love in her eyes, now that he understood the venom that existed within him.

In time, he told himself. *I just need time*.

He couldn't be sure even of that. But he had to give time a chance—had to for Marion—for himself!

The clack of hoof on stone, jerked his head to the right. There, perhaps a quarter of a mile away, moved a column of riders. *Raiding party* filled his mind and evaporated just as quickly when he discerned the wide-brimmed hats worn by each of the riders.

Militia!

There was no doubt. The riders were regular Texas militia headed toward San Antonio. Why, he didn't know.

Sands called out a greeting and reined to the right. A man's voice hailed him in reply and ordered him to ride in with hands held wide and open. Sands did as he was told, identifying himself as he moved beside the column. A sergeant met him and directed him to a Lieutenant Norwood at the head of the column.

"What in the hell's regular militia doing out here?" Sands asked after a brief greeting.

"Security," Norwood answered. "Orders from the secretary of war. We're a scouting force. A company of infantry is about a mile to the rear."

"Security?" Sands asked.

"Colonel Fisher isn't taking any chances with the Comanches," the lieutenant said. "Can't blame him none. Even if them damned redskins say they're coming in for a peace parley, I don't trust them none."

Peace Parley. The pronouncement rolled through Sands' brain. *And who is this Colonel Fisher?* He hadn't heard anything about any Comanches or a Colonel Fisher coming to San Antonio. But then, Colonel Karnes didn't tell him everything.

★TWELVE★

The morning of March 19th found Sands standing outside the ranger garrison with his mouth agape in disbelief. The startled commotion from his companions within the old bunkhouse echoed his disquiet. Running a hand over his eyes, he stared northward through the harsh yellows of the early hour. The ineffectual gesture did nothing to remove the scene or abate his surprise.

Since Colonel Fisher and a company of Texas regulars had escorted the other two members of the treaty commission—Fisher, himself, being the third member—into town three days ago, rumors had run rampant through San Antonio. Everyone was only too willing to share their speculation about Moor-war-ruh, whether he would return. Sands had suspected that the old *par-riah-boh* and his two companions would never be seen again. And if they did return, it would be at the head of a raiding party. Never in his wildest imaginings did he envision this!

Sands' mouth twisted to the right and his lips pursed tightly to spit a thin, brown stream of tobacco juice. His eyes narrowed skeptically and shifted over the Comanche camp that now was erected on the very edge of town. He spat again. The tipis were out of place this close to the buildings of San Antonio.

"Lord, there's so many of them." Will Brown walked from the garrison. "Moor-war-ruh apparently expects the council to take up some time."

"Sixty-five in all," Sands said and punctuated the remark with another expelled stream of dark brown juice.

He had counted every one of the coppery-red faces. Moor-war-ruh had brought more than two other chiefs with him this time. Twelve war chiefs rode with the *par-riahboh*. And each of those traveled with their squaws and children . . . and their dogs, mules, and horses.

Will was right; from all appearances the *Pehnahterkuh* had come for more than a morning's visit. Their camp had a look of permanence about it. A fact that boded well for the treaty council. A Comanche didn't bring his family along when raiding was on his mind.

The crunch of sand and stone beneath boots drew Sands' attention to the right. Hays, Karnes, and the Lipan Beasos approached. The three paused momentarily as they strolled toward the Comanche lodges. Sands couldn't hear the words Hays and Karnes exchanged, but Hays nodded after a few moments and walked toward the garrison.

Before Sands could inquire as to how things proceeded within town, Hays waved him off and said, "I'm not sure what's happening . . . just that it is. Karnes and I are going to take Moor-war-ruh and the other chiefs to the courthouse. The commissioners are ready to begin the council."

Sands did not comment. The Indian Commission appointed by President Lamar was a hard one—Colonel William G. Cooke, presently the acting secretary of war since Johnston had resigned for military service, Colonel Hugh McLeod, the Texas adjutant general, and Lieutenant Colonel William Fisher of the 1st Texas Regiment. All three shared the President's never-give-an-inch policy toward redmen within the republic.

Jack shook his head. "It's tense, Josh. Seems Lamar has said there will be no bartering for the return of captives. No ransoms will be paid . . ."

Sands drew a deep, uncertain breath. Presenting Indians, especially Comanches, with gifts during a council was a long established tradition. The English had begun it when they first came to Texas, and it had been continued by the French, Spanish, Mexicans, and the Texian governments.

". . . Fisher's also acting strange," Jack said, his gaze turning to the tipis. "I think he's hiding something. He won't talk about what Lamar said to him. He's like a man on needles."

Sands slowly released the breath. The standard military grapevine had been abuzz the past few days. The government's peace terms were known even to the lowest private. Peace would come if the Comanches agreed to remain west of a line drawn through Central Texas, never again approach white settlements, and not interfere with the settling of vacant lands anywhere within the republic.

The three demands sounded more like an ultimatum to Sands than contingencies for peace. However, with all the military men on the commission, he suspected the strong position was just a starting point to begin negotiations. Unless the commissioners displayed a bowed neck and a stiff spine, they'd get nowhere with the *Nermernuh*. Comanches could sense weakness in a man, and when they did, it was like a pack of wolves attacking a wounded deer. They were relentless until they had him hamstrung and helpless. Then they went for the jugular vein.

"What about captives?" Sands asked, remembering the

council had been called on Moor-war-ruh's promise to return all the Comanches' white captives.

"They've released two . . . a Mexican boy and a white girl. The girl, a Matilda Lockhart, is with a group of ladies at the Maverick home now," Hays said. "I want you two to go over there. The commission is waiting to hear a report on the girl's condition before starting the council. And, Josh, do it quick!"

Jack threw a thumb over a shoulder to emphasize "quick," then turned and rejoined Karnes who stiffly strolled toward the tipis where Moor-war-ruh and the other chiefs waited.

Sands glanced at Will who only nodded for his friend to lead the way into town.

Mary Maverick, wife of San Antonio's prominent merchant Samuel Maverick, waited for them outside her home. One glance at the petite women told Sands all was far from right. A blush of scarlet anger colored her cheeks, and distance deeply furrowed her forehead.

"By God Almighty, no human being, man or woman, should have to suffer the torments she's been through," the woman's voice came tight and strained as Sands and Will escorted her toward the town's main plaza and the courthouse. "She's only sixteen! She won't even look at the other women. She says she'll never be able to to hold her head up again after what they did to her!"

Mary Maverick hastily detailed what Matilda Lockhart had told the town ladies as the womenfolk bathed and dressed the girl after her release. Matilda and her three-year-old sister had been carried away by a raiding party in Thirty-Eight.

"Her head and arms and face are nothing but bruises and sores," the woman said. "And her nose—it's been burnt off to the bone . . . both nostrils are wide and denuded.''

As delicately as possible Mary Maverick recounted the sexual abuses the Comanche braves had heaped upon Matilda Lockhart. When they finished with the girl, she was turned over to the squaws who held torches to her face, delighting in her screams of agony. Matilda Lockhart's emaciated body now bore a myriad of scars—scars inflicted by searing tongues of flame.

Mary Maverick repeated the horrors for the commissioners when they reached the main plaza. The three listened without comment, although their eyes narrowed and their faces hardened.

"Matilda's an intelligent girl. She learned to speak Comanche," Mary Maverick concluded her second telling of Matilda Lockhart's tale of torture and degradation. "She says there were fifteen other white captives in the camp where they kept her. The savages didn't bring them here."

The seething fury that raged within the commissioners was visible in their expressions when they turned at the sound of the approaching *Pehnahterkuh* procession. Sands felt more than the tension Hays had mentioned. He could almost smell a bloodlust exuding from the three.

Surely they didn't expect anything else, Sands thought. The tortures of Indian captives, man, woman, and child alike, were well-known to all. Matilda Lockhart was the rule, not the exception. As cruel as it was, it was a reality that had to be accepted when dealing with the Comanche.

Nothing would be achieved by dwelling on what had been. The past was past, and its victims could be comforted, not reclaimed.

Today Moor-war-ruh and his chiefs had come in peace, protected by the inviolate sanctity of a treaty council. Although the commissioners might desire to right what

Matilda Lockhart had suffered, it was beyond their power. They could, however, secure the release of all the captives the *Nermernuh* presently held and assure there would be no further captives and atrocities.

Simply put, there was nothing the three could do this day except talk with Moor-war-ruh and the chiefs. However, from the unyielding granite hardness of the commissioners' faces, Sands felt any words that passed their lips would be a total waste. Matilda Lockhart's tale had killed any hope of negotiations . . . at least for today.

But then, a council this important would not be a one day event. The fact that the *Pehnahterkuh* band had erected a camp on the edge of town indicated they recognized the time that would be needed to mold a workable treaty.

Sands glanced at the Comanches. Moor-war-ruh and the twelve war chiefs filed into the white limestone courthouse. As with their first appearance in San Antonio, the braves wore only their finest regalia—long-fringed buckskins, brightly colored stone and glass beads, and eagle feathers in their long, buffalo grease-slicked hair.

Outside the courthouse the warriors' squaws, painted and also dressed in their most colorful costumes, squatted on the ground to await the return of their men. Here and there groups of young Comanche boys played at the games of their elders—war.

A large crowd of curious onlookers, white and Mexican alike, gathered close to glimpse the faces of their feared enemies. Men reached into their pockets and tossed coins to the ground as targets for the Comanche children's miniature arrows.

At least they're not hostile, Sands thought as he followed Hays and Karnes into the limestone building. The last thing this council needed was a hostile mob screaming for Indian blood. Those gathered today were merely curious, each wanting to see the strange and dreaded Comanche.

Inside, the chiefs settled cross-legged to the packed earth floor. Their dark eyes impassively watched the three commissioners and other whites who entered to stand across from them along the opposite wall of the building.

"Moor-war-ruh . . ." Colonel Cooke began as the last man walked through the open courthouse door.

Sands cringed inwardly. Cooke ignored common courtesy by immediately opening the council. The Comanche way was almost leisurely to the white. There was supposed to be a polite period of silence for all assembled to clear their minds. Then they would discuss less important matters like the weather and the buffalo herds this spring. Perhaps those who had come to council would share tobacco to show their intentions were honorable. Then and only then would the real negotiations begin.

Often this was slow and time consuming to whites, but it was the way of the *Nermernuh*, and it had to be respected if the commission hoped to achieve anything.

Cooke continued, ". . . why have you not brought more captives here as was promised when you first met with Colonel Karnes two months ago? The return of white captives was expressly given as a condition for this council."

Moor-war-ruh's bald head slowly rose. Sands detected a sadness in the old *par-riah-boh*'s eyes when they turned to Cooke, as though he mourned the loss of the courtesy due him. His gaze methodically moved along the line of whites, staring into each of the faces that gazed at him. When he spoke, it was in his own tongue. Beasos served as an interpreter quickly translating each sentence.

"My people hold no other captives. The others belonged to other bands. I do not control those camps . . ."

The great *par-riah-boh* of the Pehnahterkuh spoke

eloquently. Also elusively, Sands realized. While he was certain Moor-war-ruh did not lie, the old leader sidestepped the truth about the fifteen captives Matilda Lockhart had spoken of. While the captives might have been in Moor-war-ruh's custody they were considered the property of other bands and not in his "control." Although considered an uncivilized savage by the Texians he faced, Moor-war-ruh had the soul and silver-tongue to match any politician in the republic.

"The other camps have promised their willingness to ransom the whites they hold." Moor-war-ruh continued for thirty minutes with a detailed outline of the dry goods, ammunition, blankets, and vermilion the Comanche bands would accept for the return of the captives. He ended his lengthy oration with a single calm question. "How do you like that answer?"

Sands detected no more than the usual Comanche arrogance in Moor-war-ruh's question. He simply inquired if the demands for the captives were suitable.

The commissioners didn't like the *Pehnahterkuh*'s answer at all. Whether they read something into Moor-war-ruh's answer that wasn't there, Sands couldn't tell. But Colonel Fisher answered the *par-riah-boh* by ordering a file of infantrymen into the room.

What in hell? Sands stared incredulously as the soldiers took positions along the walls. A sentinel defiantly stood blocking the open door to the courthouse.

Like Sands, Moor-war-ruh and his chiefs stared at the soldiers and stirred restively as the uniformed men filed into the room.

Colonel Fisher leaned toward his two fellow commissioners. When the three turned back to the Comanches, it was Colonel Cooke who spoke to Beasos; he made no attempt to disguise the contempt in his voice.

"Inform Moor-war-ruh and the others that they are Colonel Fisher's prisoners by order of President Mirabeau Lamar . . . that they will be detained until every white captive held by the Comanche tribes are returned. Only after the release of the captives will it be proper to discuss . . . presents for savages. Texians will not be held for ransom!"

Beasos' deep coppery hue paled. His dark eyes grew saucer round, then narrowed to mere slits.

Sands could see the tremors of fear quake through the former Comanche captive. The Lipan Apache's head vehemently shook from side to side in refusal of Cooke's order. When he spoke, his words came clear and firm:

"You can not do that! They will not stand for it, sir. These are Comanche warriors. They will fight to the death before they allow themselves to be taken prisoner."

"Tell them, man!" Cooke was adamant; his tone was tinged with outrage that Beasos questioned his command. "I demand that you tell them every word that I said. *Every word!*"

Beasos glared at Cooke. His lips parted, but he uttered no sound.

"Tell him! Tell Moor-war-ruh everything I said!" Cooke demanded, his voice rising to a shout.

Beasos' head turned to the *Pehnahterkuh par-riah-boh*. He sucked in a deep steadying breath. His tongue nervously licked at his lips. His voice trembled, the Apache scout did as he was told. Slowly and distinctly, he translated Cooke's words—*every word*.

Then without so much as a glance to the three members of the commission, or any other man in the room, Beasos ran. He shot toward the courthouse door, shoved aside the soldier standing there, and bolted outside before anyone could react.

In the next instant, Sands and every other man in the small low-slung building completely forgot the scout.

Shrieking war cries echoed from the bare limestone walls, rebounding on themselves. Thirteen Comanche chiefs as though of one mind bounded to their feet.

No more than three strides behind Beasos, a warrior who streamed long black braids dashed after the Lipan. Sands saw a glint of silver flash in his coppery hand, only to disappear into the stomach of the sentinel barring the door. The soldier groaned, dropping his rifle as he clutched at the knife hilt that jutted from his midriff. Dark crimson welled in a flowing current from around the buried blade as his knees buckled and he collapsed face down on the packed-dirt floor.

From outside Sands heard the escaped warrior's cries of treachery as he reached the town plaza.

Then there was another voice, one from inside the courthouse—a white voice screaming out for the soldiers to open fire. Sands jerked around searching for the voice's owner; he found no one.

The soldiers responded without question. Thunder rolled through the crowded courthouse in a resounding chorus. Smoke, billowing clouds of exploding black powder, filled the room and the whine of lead ricochetted off limestone and whistled about Sands.

For the first time in his life Joshua Sands felt sheer panic. His mind refused to accept what his eyes saw. His body balked though his brain screamed for it to run for the door.

Red and white fell, cut down by the rifle balls. From the corner of an eye Sands saw fellow ranger Matthew Caldwell, who was an unarmed onlooker like himself, grab his leg. Scarlet blossomed on the thigh of his breeches. Pain and anger twisted Caldwell's face. Wounded as he was, he reached out and wrenched a rifle from the hands of a chief who darted for the unguarded door. The ranger then turned the weapon on its owner, blowing the Comanche's head away.

When Sands' eyes turned from the bloody scene, Caldwell was using the rifle's butt to batter in the face of another of the chiefs.

Across the room, Sands saw old Moor-war-ruh drive his knife into the side of Ranger Captain Tom Howard. In the next instant the *par-riah-boh* fell, cut down by one of the soldiers' rifles.

Sand's mind and body suddenly broke free of the bonds of horror that gripped them. He moved. Grabbing Will and Jack, who stood unarmed like himself, he dragged them through the courthouse door before a ricochetting rifle ball could find them—or him.

Outside was no better than within. Several of the chiefs had made their way to the plaza where their cries had aroused the fury of the Comanches who waited there.

Squaws and children fought with the same ferocity of their men. Yanking weapons away from the hands of onlookers, they turned them on the confused crowd. Miniature arrows, mere toys but a moment ago, shafted into the town's citizenry. Sands saw a circuit judge collapse with one of the small shafts jutting from his heart. He was but one of several men who paid with their lives to learn that Comanche children's arrows were just as deadly as those used by their fathers.

Soldiers stationed around the plaza answered the assault upon the crowd by lifting their rifles and opening fire. The death cries of the *Nermernuh* mingled with the thunderlike reports. The Comanches whose bodies jerked and twisted beneath the impact of rifle balls were not warriors, but squaws and their children. And like the *Pehnahterkuh* chiefs they had followed into San Antonio, they died.

"Will, get the men!" Hays cried out, waving the young ranger toward the garrison. "And bring our weapons! And hurry the hell about it!"

Will didn't question, just ran.

Unarmed, and his stomach threatening to empty itself, Sands stood by Hays' side. Until Will returned, all that either could do was stare on in mute horror as the streets of San Antonio ran red.

★THIRTEEN★

Sands watched four soldiers drag the squaw from the jail. He wasn't certain of her name, only that she had been one of the wives of the dead *Pehnahterkuh* war chief Many Ponies. In spite of the grasping arms that wrenched her to one side then to the other, she appeared passive and uncaring. Only the ice in her coal-black eyes hinted at the hate that seethed within her breast and brain.

Sands saw the same hatred reflected in the faces of soldiers and onlookers who crowded about the small jail, heard it growled in their throats and voices. If there had been a chance for peace—even a temporary one between redman and white—it had been rent asunder. The Comanche refusal to release their captives had irreparably violated the very foundations of the peace council for whites, while Fisher's soldiers and the treacherous attack had breeched the *Nermernuh*'s sacred sanctuary of a council meeting.

Thirty-five *Pehnahterkuh* had died in the fighting—braves, women, and children. Seven whites had fallen and another ten had been seriously injured. No one had bothered to count the minor wounds suffered by the onlookers—or the Comanche.

The thirty-two Indian survivors—all squaws and children—had been seized and packed into the confines of a jail that was little more than a single cell made from limestone blocks. San Antonio now placed itself behind bars of its own. The majority of the citizenry remained behind locked and barred doors, with loaded rifles in terrified hands. The whole town was abuzz with rumors of Comanche reprisals for the "Council House Fight," as the massacre had been dubbed overnight.

"Tell her to ride to the camps of her people and spread the word of how the republic now deals with liars, murderers and butchers." Colonel Fisher's voice drew Sands' attention back to to the soldiers and their prisoner.

The soldiers lifted the squaw astride the bare back of a mustang mare. Her eyes never leaving her captors, she took the single hackamore rein in a steady hand while Beasos translated Fisher's words. Then she securely gathered a bundle of food a soldier handed her into the crook of her free arm.

"Tell her to inform her people that unless the Comanche bands release all their white captives within twelve days, the prisoners we now hold will be put to death," Fisher ordered the Lipan scout.

Beasos did as told with a doubtful shake of his head; the soldiers released the squaw when Fisher nodded to them. She rode from town as passively as she had been pulled from the jail.

Sands turned away sucking at his teeth. The squaw's facade was deceptive. The cries of the mourning chant she would wail when she reached her band already echoed in his mind. Those cries of sorrow and rage would soon be heard all across the plains—of that he was certain.

* * *

Listlessly, Sands stirred a fork among the pinto beans and bacon that filled the tin plate balanced on his knee. He tried to listen to Hays, but his mind, like those of every man in the garrison, refused to give up the bloody visions of yesterday's council meeting. Even the heat radiating from the black box stove he sat beside provided no warmth. It might be late March—spring this far south in Texas— but today seemed colder than the days of the winter.

The bunkhouse was silent for several heavy minutes after Jack concluded his announcement. Sands lifted a forkful of beans toward his mouth, then dropped it back to the plate. In spite of his stomach's rumbling, he had lost whatever appetite he had. He placed the plate on the floor beside the chair, and looked up at Jack.

"No patrols for twelve days, huh?"

"Karnes' orders," Jack said with a dubious heave of his chest. "He says we are to respect the word as well as the intent of Fisher's command. Give the Comanches the chance to return the captives. Karnes said that he feels even reconnaissance patrol could be interpreted as a hostile action."

"Hostile action! Bullshit!" this from Hap Ingram.

Twelve days without patrols was insanity! Sands silently cursed Karnes' and Fisher's parental relationship to a female dog. If either man knew what he was doing, he'd send out the soldiers with the rangers. Let them attack before the bands could recover from the loss of their chiefs. That would drive home the point in the only language the *Nermernuh* understood—blood!

Jack shrugged. "For the next twelve days we're stuck here. Until Karnes changes his mind, everyone's on repair duty. That means new roofs for the stable, then the garrison."

The men just sat there, not even protesting the order with the usual chorus of disgruntled moans.

"You got a Joshua Sands in here?" A soldier opened the door and poked his head inside. "There's a wagon out here and the driver wants to talk with a Joshua Sands."

Jack glanced at Sands then motioned him to the door with a tilt of his head. Sands rose and walked through the still open door.

The wagon outside was the Hammer wagon. Marion and Jamie sat beside a heavy set man with a thick shock of salt and pepper hair that pushed in disarray from beneath a weather-beaten hat.

"Mr. Sands," the man called out and stretched a hand down from the driver's seat toward the ranger, "the name's Arlan Turner. I'm Marion's father . . . and this boy's grandfather."

The man tossled Jamie's hair and smiled as Sands took his proffered hand and shook it. "Marion told me all you did for her and my grandson after . . . after what happened to Felix. I didn't think it would be right for me to head back to Linnville without at least telling you how much your kindness is appreciated."

"Linnville?" Sands' gaze shot to Marion. Her green eyes rolled downward as though embarrassed; guilt suffused Sands. "You're leaving for Linnville?"

"Thought we could make thirty or forty miles 'fore sundown," Arlan Turner said. "After what happened here yesterday, it don't seem safe to loiter around San Antonio any more than necessary. The sooner I get my daughter and grandson back to the coast, the safer I'll feel."

Sands looked back at Marion. For an instant her eyes rose to him expectantly. Words, the desire to call to her, to ask her to stay, formed on Sands' tongue. Then a bitterness like bile rose within him to drown his unspoken words.

The expectancy in Marion's face faded, and her gaze returned to the ground. Sands could see the hurt that trembled at the corners of her mouth: hurt that he placed there. He cursed himself for that, but could not utter the words that would erase the pain.

Sands' brow furrowed as he turned back to Marion's father. "You aren't thinking about heading out alone, are you?"

Arlan Turner shook his head. "I brought three other supply wagons with me up from Linnville. They're waiting at the other side of town for me."

Sands nodded his approval. Usually the journey from San Antonio to the coast was safe enough for a single wagon, but now, after all that had happened, the only safety was in numbers.

"S'pect it would be best for a man to drive straight south," Arlan Turner said. "Put as much distance between the wagon and San Antonio as possible before turning east."

"That'd be my advice, Mr. Turner," Sands said. "Keep an eye on your team and wagon. It's not a time to have either break down."

"Aye." Arlan Turner held out his hand once more and shook Sands' again. "Reckon we'd best be going. Thank you again, Mr. Sands, for all the aid you've given Marion and Jamie."

"Marion . . ." Sands started, feeling himself open to the woman, then the words vanished when her head lifted. All he could mumble was, "Marion, you keep care of yourself. And Jamie, you look after you mother, hear?"

"I'm the man of the family now, Josh." Jamie grinned widely, his small chest expanding. "I'll watch after Ma."

Sands' gaze shifted back to Marion as her father lifted the reins. He saw moisture welling around her emerald eyes, but there were no tears.

"And you, Joshua Sands," she said, "you take care of yourself."

"Aye," Arlan Turner said. "Should you ever meander down Linnville way, know that the door to my house is open to you—day or night."

With that, the man lifted his whip and snaked it out so that it popped loudly above the team leader's head, while he whistled and called out to the horses. The wagon creaked as its thick-spoked wheels began to turn.

As Sands stood mutely staring up, Marion's lips silently formed the three words he had been unable to say to her—"I love you."

Then the wagon moved away, and she and Jamie and her father were gone from his sight, hidden by the canvas covering the wagon's bed. Deriding himself, Sands watched the wagon roll southward behind a line of white-washed buildings.

His head jerked around and he stared at the ranger stable. There was still time to saddle up and ride after them. Time to ask Marion to remain—to make a life with him.

Sands looked at the garrison, then back at the stable, unable to bring himself to take that first step, unable to ride after the woman he loved.

The retreating wagon with Arlan Turner at the reins offered him an unexpected solution to all the questions and doubts that had plagued his brain. It was the coward's way out, he realized, but he took it.

Seven days after the Council House Fight, a cry went up from a sentry, bringing Sands and Will scrambling down from their awkward perch atop the rangers' stable. Their gazes followed the soldier's pointing finger northward until they located the source of the man's excitement—a cloud of dust—and before it a lone man riding hell bent for leather straight for town.

Jack and the remainder of the company had joined them by the time the rider reached the garrison. The man wasn't a man, but a woman who identified herself as Catherine Webster. Nestled securely in her arms was an infant daughter.

"I got away!" Tears of joy transformed to mud as they streamed down her dust covered cheeks. "My lord, I didn't think I could do it. I thought they'd catch up with me and kill us both. They've gone crazy! They're killing all the whites. All of them! Don't you understand? All of them!"

The woman's eyes were saucer round and wild. Her words came in a disjointed rhythm, and her meaning, if any, was lost on Sands.

Under Jack's direction the hysterical woman was guided into the garrison and given coffee. After three steaming cups, drained in hasty gulps without a single sound except her own heavy breathing, she looked up at the men who pressed around her.

"I stole me a horse while they were killing everybody. I got my baby, but I couldn't get to Booker. They took him from me, but they didn't kill him like they did all the other whites. They had already made him a Comanche . . . made him one of their adopted sons. But they killed all the rest. They would have killed us if I hadn't stole the horse," Catherine Webster's sentences still came fast and jerky as though she couldn't get them out quickly enough.

"Comanches," Jack asked, "did they attack your wagons . . . farm?"

"No, no," the woman shook her head violently. "We was captives. My baby, my son . . . Booker . . . and me. But I escaped. Got away before they could kill us like they was doing to all the others. They only spared Booker and the Putnam girl 'cause they was adopted . . . the Comanches had made them part of their tribe."

Jack poured the woman another cup of coffee, then turned to Hank Ferris and ordered him to gather some of the town's women and bring them to the garrison to care for Mrs. Webster. He sent Hap Ingram to inform Colonel Karnes of the woman's escape from the Comanche. Jack then pulled a chair beside her and in a soft and gentle voice began to piece together her story.

She had escaped from a *Pehnahterkuh* band a day ago and ridden south toward San Antonio, certain the Comanche would follow her and her young daughter.

"They went crazy about three days before that," Mrs. Webster said. "Best I could tell was that some of their chiefs had been killed here in San Antonio . . ."

She told of braves and squaws wailing and screaming all through the night.

"They tore at their faces, chopped off fingers. The squaws were even ripping at their teats," she said. "Most of the men cut off their hair and sat on the ground moaning and crying like children."

Sands could not suppress the icy floe that moved up his spine. Their long black tresses were sacred to the Comanche, both men and women, to shave their scalps was unheard of. He had no doubt that their insane grief stemmed from news of the Council House Fight.

"I'm not certain how long it all went on," Mrs. Webster continued. "But when the wailing ended, there was only fire in their eyes. And those eyes were on the captives they held in the camp."

One by one, the band took each of the captives and staked them naked to the ground outside the camp, she detailed. "They mutilated them. Cut the skin from their bodies. And when the men were through, the squaws burned them with torches and embers from the fires, laughing at the screams."

Catherine Webster looked up at the men around her. "There weren't no men captives. Only young women and children. But that didn't make no difference. They killed them. When they came for the little Lockhart girl, I made my break."

Sands was certain that the Lockhart girl, Mrs. Webster spoke of was Matilda Lockhart's sister. The girl was only six years old. She had been tortured by Comanche knives, then her mutilated body was burned alive while her screams rose helplessly to the heavens.

"Captain, there's some ladyfolks outside," Hap was back with Karnes at his side.

While Jack reiterated Mrs. Webster's story for the colonel, Will and two other rangers took the woman outside to those offering comfort for her and her child.

"We need to get word of this to Colonel Fisher," Karnes said.

"Might be better if he and his men moved back into town instead of holing up in San José Mission," Jack suggested.

Karnes shook his head. "I don't think that'll happen. Fisher's taken sick. He says the mission, with its walls, is a natural made prison for the Comanche captives."

Sands tuned the men out. He didn't care what Fisher wanted; the military colonel had made his move. Now *Pehnahterkuh* had begun to exact retribution for Fisher's murder of their chiefs. And Sands feared the captives who had died were only the first payment.

★FOURTEEN★

"I don't understand! Where are they?" Will Brown yanked off his hat back and swiped at his forehead with the arm of his shirt. Tiny droplets of sweat immediately popped out on his brow to replace those wiped away. "They can't just up and disappear. Can they?"

Sands shook his head and shrugged. It wasn't an answer, but he didn't have any answers. At least none that made any sense.

He searched the open prairie that fanned wide below the patrol. Even from the vantage point atop the rise, he saw nothing except grass and rock baking in an already hot morning sun. He had given up trying to make sense of the vast emptiness two weeks ago. Like everything since the Council House Fight back in March, nothing seemed to fit together the way it was supposed to.

The Comanche revenge he feared had come. Three days before the end of Fisher's twelve-day truce *Pehnahterkuh* bands had ridden on San Antonio and surrounded the town. They had the numbers and the strength to raze the town. Yet, they didn't attack; they merely rode about taunting the soldiers with shouted insults and challenges for Fisher's men to ride forth and face them in hand-to-hand combat.

What could have been a massacre had been diverted by one fact: the *Pehnahterkuh* had no leader to unite them—all their powerful chiefs had been killed in the council house.

The ineffectual display of Comanche bravado might have been seen as a joke by some, had it not been for the steady wave of raiding parties. The *Nermernuh* struck the frontier with an unheard of ferocity and brutality that paralyzed the southwestern region with terror. Night or day, the Comanches were always there.

The rangers had been unable to contain the attacks; there had been too many for such a small company. Jack Hays had answered the need for men by organizing what he called his "Minute Men." The pealing of the San Fernando church bell and the raising of the flag over San Antonio's courthouse now brought a troop of town volunteers running to aid the ranger captain and his troop.

The "Minute Men" helped, Sands admitted, though they had not been enough. Even with the extra men from nearby communities that organized their own "Minute Men" companies, it had been only a defensive measure. The rangers had never been able to take the offensive against the raiding *Pehnahterkuh*.

The government sent regular army to aid in the fighting. While the Texian infantry could stand without shame against the troops of Mexico, when it came to Indian fighting, they were useless.

The Comanche avoided direct confrontation with the army. And there was no way a foot soldier could effectively pursue an enemy who was borne on horseback.

As for the *Pehnahterkuh* squaws and children taken at the Council House Fight . . . Sands sadly shook his head. They were the only real joke stemming from the situation.

A few had been traded for the return of Mrs. Webster's son Booker and two other Comanche captives.

The rest?

Fisher might have been fool enough to breech a peace council, but he was wasn't cold-blooded. His originally ordered execution of the captives was never carried out. Instead the squaws and children had been given to townsfolk as "servants."

Sands sucked at his teeth. Servant in this case was just another word for slave.

However, no Comanche, not even a child, would bow his neck to a white man's yoke. After a few weeks of "servanthood" every one of the *Pehnahterkuh* had escaped from San Antonio. Often they rode back to their prairie bands astride a horse stolen from their "employees." Even the Mexican boy who had been released with Matilda Lockhart had stolen away and rejoined a Comanche band.

Then, in early summer, the raids stopped.

Ranger patrol after ranger patrol rode out and returned never seeing a sign of a Comanche, or their camps. Indian scouts reported the *Pehnahterkuh* had withdrawn to the high plains with its massive herds of great hump-backed buffalo.

Now as dawn rose on the sixth day of August, Sands and the patrol of five men he led only found the hot Texas sun challenged their right to ride the prairie. So it had been for seven weeks.

"Josh," Clay Poteet, one of the San Antonio "Minute Men," called out and handed Sands a slim, brass, collapsible telescope. "About a quarter of a mile to the east. What do you make of it?"

Opening the spyglass, Sands held it to his right eye and scanned the area Clay pointed toward. Nothing, he saw nothing but prairie. What did Clay expect him to . . .

Sands caught his breath. There, exactly where Clay had indicated, the ground was tramped as though an army had moved through. Lowering, the glass, he looked back at the man.

"Comanche?" Clay asked.

"It wasn't there three days ago when the patrol passed this way. And there ain't no buffalo herds that big this far south." Sands reined his mount toward the east, using his heels to nudge the gelding into an easy gallop.

The rest of the patrol followed, stopping when they reached the wide swath of trampled ground. Sands swung to the ground and knelt. His right hand tentatively reached out to one of the tracks. When he looked up, his forehead was furrowed with deep lines of concern.

"Unshod mustang ponies. It's Comanche all right. And lots of 'em." Sands stood and stared over the wide trail. There was trampled ground for at least a quarter of a mile to the east, and it stretched as far as the eye could see to the north and south. "They moved through here at least two days ago heading south."

He understated the situation. A quarter mile swath of tracks indicated more than "lots" of Comanche. Hundreds of *Nermernuh*, astride their mustangs, had ridden through here undetected—and they were headed south. They had penetrated the frontier border and now rode directly into the heart of unsuspecting settled Texas!

For a long, silent moment, Sands stood, his gaze lost in the open land to the south. He could only guess at the actual number of the Comanche; there were simply too many hoof prints for an accurate estimate. He glanced back at his men. Their worry-wrinkled brows said they shared his thoughts—and those weren't pretty!

"I've got to warn Ben McCulloch over in Gonzales,"

Sands said as he stepped back into the saddle. "Will, I want you to ride with me."

Will nodded.

"Bill, Jim, we'll need extra mounts. Double with Sam and Howard and ride back to the garrison. Tell Hays what we've seen. Tell him what we've done."

The men did as ordered, stripping their mounts of saddles and bridles, then climbing on behind their companions. Looping ropes about the free animals' necks, Sands and Will tightened their holds and eased their own horses into an easy lope. As soon as the horses they led matched the pace, they urged their mounts into a gallop, then a full run on a course straight for Gonzales.

If need be, they'd ride their own mounts until they dropped, then saddle the borrowed horses and ride on. It was an old Comanche trick, one that allowed the braves to cover a hundred miles in a single night if need be. It was a trick Sands hoped would prevent those same braves from laying waste the vulnerable heartland of settled Texas.

Sands gave one quick glance over his shoulder to the four men who rode double back to San Antonio, then turned his full attention to the trail ahead.

They found Captain Ben McCulloch three hours later as he pulled a saddle from a lathered mount outside the Gonzales garrison.

"Hays' men, huh?" McCulloch responded to Sands' quick introduction. "Does Jack know that it looks like all hell's broken loose? It looks like a whole damn army of *Pehnahterkuh* are moving on Victoria!"

"Victoria?" this from Will, who glanced wide-eyed to Sands then back to McCulloch. "That's eighty miles from here. They're moving that fast?"

McCulloch's eyebrow lifted. "Then Jack knows?"

"He should, by now," Sands answered and hastily reported the quarter-mile wide trail they had ridden upon that morning. "I sent the rest of the men with me back to San Antonio to tell Captain Hays what we'd seen, then rode here to warn you."

McCulloch nodded and threw a blanket and saddle on a fresh horse one of his men led from the stable. "I appreciate what you've done. But damn, I wish you'd brought every man in San Antonio. Ain't no doubt it's Comanches that cut the trail. And it ain't no raiding party! From what I've seen it looks like every buck from the plains is riding right through Texas."

McCulloch then explained he had ridden across the trail earlier that morning. "Followed it for ten miles. They hit the Johnson place . . . 'bout two days ago if I make the signs correctly. Killed Tom and his wife and their three young'uns. The two milk cows had been butchered, and the string of horses Tom kept were gone, stolen. Not much left of the place except ashes."

McCulloch looked at Sands then Will and shook his head, then he reached beneath the horse's belly to get the girth that hung there.

"Any plans?" Sands asked.

McCulloch slipped the clinch through the girth and pulled it tight. He popped a hand against the horse's belly and pulled the leather strap even tighter. "Ain't much I can do. I got two dozen men here in Gonzales. Twenty-four men ain't enough to go charging off after a Comanche army that's at least two days ahead of us."

"You've got to do something!" Will protested.

"I intend to," McCulloch said as he tied off the clinch. "First thing I plan to do is draft you two boys into my company. Ain't no use for you to go riding back to San Antonio when you're needed here."

"But Captain Hays . . ." Will started.

"Would do the same if he was in my place," McCulloch cut him off. "I need men and you two are warm bodies."

Sands and Will both nodded their acceptance to McCulloch's stern gaze.

"Good," McCulloch edged back his hat. "My men are scattered all round here now, trying to round up every able bodied man they can. As soon as they get back, we'll be riding toward Victoria, keeping to the Comanches' flanks. Like I said, there ain't much a handful of men can do against an army. The way I see it, we can keep at their heels and bury the dead they leave behind."

McCulloch paused. "I got riders out to some of the other ranger companies in the area. They'll send out the call the same as me. But we need the time to gather our strength."

"What I need now is scouts, men to stay on them bucks' asses and keep me informed of what's happening," McCulloch said. "That's what you two will be doing. I want you two as close to them butchers as possible, and I want to know their every move. If one of 'em picks his nose, I want to know about it. Understand?"

Again Sands nodded and Will followed suit.

"That's good, because scouting is all I want. Until we got the men to stand against whatever made that trail, I don't want no foolishness. At no time are you to engage the Comanche. And that, my friends, ain't gonna be easy," McCulloch said. " 'Cause if you're as close to them as I want you, you're going to see things that'll turn your gut inside out. Things no man could just stand by and watch. But you're going to have to do just that. Watch! And that'll be a damn sight harder to do than acting the hero and getting yourself killed!"

McCulloch paused, his gaze coolly sizing up Sands and

Will. When neither protested, he nodded and continued, "By sundown, we should have riders out in front of the Comanche, warning them that's in their path. We ain't going to be able to get to them all, but we'll get the majority. Saving lives is the best we can do until we gather the men to face the *Pehnahterkuh*."

Easing the reins over his horse's neck, McCulloch swung into the saddle and looked down at the two. "If there's no questions, I've got work that needs doing."

"Just one," Sands said. "Any idea who we're up against?"

"Only rumors," the ranger captain answered. "A couple of Tonkawa scouts picked up word a few weeks back that a *Pehnahterkuh* calling himself Buffalo Hump was trying to unite the Comanche bands. The Kiowa they got that from said Buffalo Hump didn't pull much weight with the other bands. However, the *Pehnahterkuh* were listening to him."

Buffalo Hump, Sands had never heard of the brave.

"There's fresh mounts in the stable," McCulloch said. "Pick yourself two and get on with what needs doing!"

Ten minutes later, Sands and Will were riding southward toward Victoria.

★FIFTEEN★

Five braves squatted on their haunches beneath a stand of three lofty oaks. They wore breechclouts and moccasins only; their faces, arms, chests, and legs bore wide bands of red and black—the *Nermernuh* paints of war. A gallon stoneware jug was passed from hand to hand among the five. Except for the time needed to swill down a mouthful of the home-distilled corn liquor in the jug, the *Pehnahterkuh* never stopped talking and laughing.

The objects of their amusement were two captives!

Sands' gaze shifted beyond the oaks' cool shade. There, staked spread-eagle on the ground, were a man and woman no older than the ranger. Both had been stripped naked to feel the full effects of slow broiling under the unforgiving August sun.

From the blistery red of their bodies, it appeared as if the Comanches had kept the two staked out for most of the day. Here and there, Sands saw thin trickles of crimson mingle with the sheen of sweat covering the man and woman—blood that flowed from tiny cuts in their flesh.

The knife wounds weren't serious, just deep enough to create constant agony as salt from perspiration entered the open wounds. It was the kind of never-ceasing pain that could slowly rob a man, or a woman, of his wits and eventually shatter his sanity. But then the braves didn't want to kill these two . . . at least, not quickly. They wanted to draw out the dying as long as possible, devising as much anguish as they could in that time.

"How many are there?" Will whispered as he leaned close to Sands.

"Five . . . used to be eight." Sands answered and passed the small telescope to his friend. He shifted his weight and removed a jagged-edged rock that pressed into his thigh as he lay belly-down in high grass. "There's three dead near the door to the cabin."

Will raised the spyglass and focused on the farm below. "The man and woman are still alive!"

"The braves are just cooking 'em a bit now. Come dark, they'll start getting serious. Suspect that the three dead were brothers or uncles or some family relation to the other five. The braves want to be certain the two are fully repaid for killing the others," Sands said. "They'll take their time with those two. Make them last all night."

Will lowered the telescope and turned to Sands. His jaw was firmly clenched and his face had visibly paled. "And we're supposed to ride on and let them die like that?"

" 'Under no circumstances are you to engage the Comanche'—that's what McCulloch said."

Sands peered through the spyglass again. Except for hunting knives, the warriors had neatly piled their rifles, bows, lances, and shields against the trunk of an oak ten yards from the captives. *Nermernuh* superstition, he realized. If a brave allowed his weapons too close to a woman, they could be contaminated and lose their medicine. That bit of superstition might be bad-medicine in itself.

Carefully scanning the terrain surrounding the farm, Sands searched for a hint of other *Pehnahterkuh* in the area. All he saw was lush coastal vegetation: trees, tall with great branching limbs, and high grass, green and rich. There was a world of difference here so close to the Gulf of Mexico compared to the rugged hill country around San Antonio—and only a day's hard ride separated the two.

He repeated his methodical search of the area for a second and third time. *Nothing*. And that boded well. Odds were that the five braves were stragglers fallen back from the main body of Comanche, who had ridden on to Victoria ten miles to the south. *Revenge can make a fool of man—white or red*.

Sands lowered the telescope and glanced over his shoulder. The sun sat on the western horizon; within an hour it would be dark. If the braves held true to form, they'd build a campfire before they began the slow torture of the couple below.

The night and a blazing campfire were what he needed to pull off the plan that germinated in his mind.

"Of course, McCulloch never said anything about defending ourselves if we happened to stumble on to a raiding party," Sands said and explained his scheme.

Will smiled as he listened in silent approval of Sands' plan.

A woman's scream jerked both their heads around.

Through the spyglass, Sands saw a grinning brave with knife in hand rise from beside the woman and move toward the man. A dark line of crimson oozed across the white mounds of her naked breasts. Her head, dark curls plastered against the side of her face, lay unmoving against her arm, and her eyes were closed.

Fainted, Sands sighed as he lowered the telescope. *It'll make the wait till night easier for her*.

He didn't look back when he heard a second scream—

that of a man. Until dark there was nothing he could do, except wait.

Colts cocked and held ready, Sands and Will moved their mounts at an easy walk toward the blazing campfire and the five silhouettes squatted about it.

"Ready?" Sands glanced away long enough to catch Will's nod. Then he leveled the pistol before him. "Let's burn 'em with powder!"

Sands' heels dug into his mount's flanks; the horse bolted forward. In twenty strides, the bay he had gotten in Gonzales was amid the five braves. The thunder of an exploding Colt roared over the hiss and crackle of the campfire. Will's pistol barked in answer.

Three of the five died before they could rise; the repeating pistols opened dark holes in the back of their skulls. The remaining two did manage to stand . . . and turn . . . to be greeted by the yellow-blue blaze of fire spit point blank from the barrels of rangers' pistols into their surprised faces.

Then it was over; less than a minute had passed and five Comanche braves had joined their three companions in death.

Sands swung from the saddle and waved Will to the house. "Bring soap and water to wash these wounds! Also see if you can find any lard or butter. These two are as red as boiled crawdads!"

Their names were John Lee and Carolina Davis. They had been warned of the oncoming Comanche horde by a fellow farmer that morning and had been gathering a few personal items before fleeing to Victoria when thirty *Pehnahterkuh* had ridden down on their farm.

"Kilt one with my rifle, then we holed up in the cabin,"

John Lee said while coating his wife's sun-blistered skin with butter. "The majority of 'em rode on. But seven stayed. Kilt two more 'fore three busted through the slats on the roof . . ."

"We knew we were dead then," Carolina said from beneath the blanket that now cloaked her nakedness. "We just weren't certain how long it would take for them to kill us."

Sands and Will listened to the couple's recounting while husband and wife tended each other's wounds and smeared butter over their sun-broiled bodies. The knife cuts were shallow and would heal long before either forgot this day—if they ever did.

When the husband and wife had dressed, Sands and Will escorted them to a thick woods a quarter of a mile from their cabin. They left them there in the leafy branches of a towering oak. Sands realized neither would sleep on such precarious perches, but they would be safe from any wandering bands of Comanche who might stumble upon them.

Five miles to the south, Sands halted. The cracking reports of gunfire came out of the darkness, sounding like the sharp snap of a bullwhip in the distance.

"Best stay here for the night," Sands said to Will. "If we get any closer, we might amble into the whole damned band without knowing it."

Fifteen minutes later, the two rangers had hidden their mounts in a bushy stand of cherry holly. For themselves, they found the thick branches of a sweetgum tree.

Sands sat with legs straddling a dangerously small limb of a short-needled pine. His left arm was hooked around an equally weak-looking branch just above his head. The top of a pine wasn't exactly made for a man accustomed to the wide seat of a Mexican-made saddle, but it, and the telescope, did provide the view he needed. And from what he saw, he realized there would be no better view of Victoria until Buffalo Hump moved the *Pehnahterkuh* on.

"Can you make out anything?" Will's voice came from ten feet below.

"McCulloch wanted us on Buffalo Hump's heels and that's exactly where we are," Sands answered. "Victoria's about a mile to the south. I can see the whole town and most of the surrounding lands."

The town itself appeared to be untouched by the Comanches, who rode in a wide circle about the wooden buildings as though they were a small herd of buffalo. The same could not be said for the outlying land.

Even at this distance, Sands saw the smoking rubble of cabins and houses that had been burned during the night. Scattered on the ground were the bodies of black slaves, cut down while they had been working the fields. The bloating carcasses of cows and oxen, Comanche lances jutting from their sides, littered the countryside.

It was easy for Sands to imagine what had occurred. While he and Will had been in Gonzales, Buffalo Hump and his united *Pehnahterkuh* had already reached Victoria. They had descended upon the town without warning, killing those caught in the fields on its outskirts, and slaughtering the livestock they found. Except for the horses and mules—those, the Comanche had herded together south of the town. Horses and mules were a sign of *Nermernuh* wealth; those they would never kill.

That had been just enough time for the townspeople to barricade their streets and homes.

The Comanche could have ridden into town were it not for their superstitious aversion for buildings. While they would readily attack a lone house or cabin, they saw white towns with their proliferation of stout buildings as bad medicine and shied from them.

Instead of riding through Victoria's streets and burning the buildings to the ground, they formed a magic circle around the town. The shots Sands had heard last night had been the *Pehnahterkuh* riding about Victoria, trying to work medicine against the buildings—a magic that had no effect on the still standing walls.

Through the spyglass, Sands once more scanned the terrain around Victoria. A soft whistle escaped his pursed lips. The fact that so many *Pehnahterkuh* had banded together was unheard of—but *this* revealed just how confident Buffalo Hump was of success in his brazen incursion into the white lands.

There just beyond the herd of horses and mules, on the edge of a thick wood, Sands could see the conical forms of tipis. Around the tents of buffalo hide, he saw squaws and children. A Comanche purposely didn't expose his family to danger. The presence of women and children meant but one thing—the *Pehnahterkuh* didn't expect to face a *Tejano* force—Buffalo Hump had carefully planned this unexpected strike into the unprotected heart of settled Texas.

"How many do you make 'em to be?" Will's voice drew Sands from his thoughts.

"Eight hundred . . . maybe a thousand," Sands answered. The number was more ominous when it was given the reality of words. "It's hard to tell. They're spread out around the town."

He quickly detailed for Will all that he could see and then added his speculation as to what had happened in Victoria yesterday. He breathed a silent sigh of relief when Will, with youthful enthusiasm, volunteered to ride back to McCulloch with the information.

Sands watched his companion carefully pick his way

down the lofty pine, mount, and ride northward. Unless there were more bands of stragglers like the braves at the Davis place, Will would have an unobstructed ride, Sands thought as he turned his attention back to Victoria and the army of *Nermernuh* holding it under siege.

An hour, two, three, he lost all track of time as he watched the Comanche ride in endless circles about the town. His arms and legs, which had ached and cramped in their unnatural positions around the limbs, had gone numb when the *Pehnahterkuh* broke their magic circle.

Once more lifting the collapsible telescope, Sands peered toward the tipis where a heaping pile of dry branches was set afire. Perhaps a hundred war-painted riders filed by the blaze and accepted the flaming brands the squaws held out to them.

Sands shifted his weight a bit to the left. Buffalo Hump apparently had recognized the uselessness of the magic circle and now was ready to try a different tactic against the town and the people barricaded within its buildings.

Twenty of the mounted warriors charged the town. Sands could see their mouths twisted wide, though their war cries did not carry to his treetop position.

The hastily made torches were the Comanches' new line of offense. The braves drove their ponies right up to the buildings of Victoria and flung the flaming limbs upward to the roofs of the wooden buildings.

In answer, townsmen concealed on those very roofs replied with a volley of rifle fire that echoed up to Sands' pine tree perch. Here and there, braves jerked rigidly then tumbled from the bare backs of the mustangs as rifle balls took their toll. But rifles were not enough to stop the next wave of torch-slinging warriors, or the next, or the next.

With the tenth wave, Sands saw flames licking toward the sky from a wood-shingled roof of a home on the west side of town. Three men and two women darted from the house's rear door in an attempt to reach the safety of a neighbor's home. Comanche war lances cruelly ended their flight before they had cleared ten yards.

The waves of warriors and burning limbs continued: the Victoria rifles meeting each charge. Three more houses caught fire and another five townspeople died as the Comanches rode down upon them.

The sun hung high in the sky when the the last wave of warriors threw their torches high. Then it was over. To Sands' surprise, the *Pehnahterkuh* abruptly withdrew from the town. Within a half hour, the tipis were dismantled and the Comanche army was once more on the move, heading toward the Guadalupe River and Peach Creek beyond.

Through the telescope, Sands watched as the hundreds of Indians spread outward in a great crescent. Four years before, Santa Anna's Mexican soldiers had used a similar formation as they marched through Texas, leaving a smoldering trail of destruction in their wake.

McCulloch's words echoed in Sands' brain as he worked his way down the lofty pine—*best we can do is stay on their heels and bury the dead*. There would be hundreds of dead unless McCulloch made good his promise to send riders out ahead of the *Pehnahterkuh* and warn settlers of the advancing army.

Peach Creek!

Sands froze as he reached the base of the pine. Buffalo Hump no longer led his united band southeasterly. He had turned toward the north on a direct course for the Gulf of Mexico and Lavaca Bay.

Marion!

Sitting on Lavaca Bay was a small port community that had been established as a supply route for San Antonio—a town named after its main importer John Linn—a town called Linnville. There, living with her father Arlan Turner, was Marion Hammer and her son Jamie.

A silent prayer that Buffalo Hump would once again change course, moved over Sands' lips as he swung into the saddle and spurred his mount toward Victoria.

★SIXTEEN★

Sands warily surveyed the lush vegetation around him. Since leaving Victoria, Buffalo Hump had developed a sudden, cautious respect for Texians. The war chief no longer pushed his army of *Pehnahterkuh* through settled Texas at the harried pace he had employed after breeching the frontier.

Now several bands of rear scouting parties combed the trail behind the massive column. Yesterday, Sands had barely avoided detection on several occasions. Only the dense, overgrown brush had sheltered him. Today, with the salty smell of the sea carried on the easterly breeze, he was constantly alert for the rear scouts. Yet, in the two hours since dawn, he had seen no trace of Buffalo Hump's flanking outriders.

That was until now!

Sands glanced at the body laying face down in the high grass. With his right hand resting on the butt of his Colt, he eased from the saddle and stepped beside the corpse.

The body was that of a middle-aged man, a farmer who had not been warned of the marching Comanche in all likelihood. He was naked: either stripped by the *Pehnahterkuh* or dragged from his bed early this morning. The soles of his feet had been sliced away by hunting knives. The bloody pulp that remained told a grisly tale. The man had been forced to run mile upon mile after the Comanche knives had done their terrible work.

Sands knelt and rolled the man to his back. His stomach churned violently, threatening to upheave, and his head jerked away from the gruesome visage. Slowly, with forced determination, Sands drew a deep breath, and another, another, another. The rumblings of his belly quelled, and he turned back to the corpse.

Death had come to this nameless man in the form of a rifle shot to his forehead—a blast that had ripped away a quarter of his skull. But only after the Comanche had forced him to suffer their greatest of degradations. They had cut away his genitals and stuffed them into his screaming mouth.

Hand still on the Colt, Sands rose. What this man had done to incur the wrath of the *Pehnahterkuh* no one would ever know. Perhaps he had just been in the wrong place at the wrong time, or maybe he had killed several braves before he was caught and tortured. While Sands silently hoped it was the latter, it didn't matter, not now. This man was just another body for McCulloch to bury along with the countless others Buffalo Hump had left in his wake.

Sands stepped back to his mount and pulled himself into the saddle. He felt old and tired as the full weight of the past two days pressed down around him.

Two days . . . only two days, he questioned himself.

Surely a century had passed since McCulloch had sent Will and him riding after Buffalo Hump. He pushed through the cottony fog blanketing his mind. They had ridden into Gonzales on the morning of August sixth. They caught up with the *Pehnahterkuh* in Victoria yesterday—that was the seventh. Which made today August eighth—two days . . . only two days.

In those two days and nights, he had not slept. Nor had he eaten more than a few curls of jerked beef, washed down with water from his canteen.

A hot meal would be nice. More than that he needed sleep. If Will were here, he'd risk a few hours sleep while his friend stood guard. But Will wasn't here: Will was . . .

For a few confused moments he couldn't remember where Will had gone. Then he recalled his friend volunteering to ride back to McCulloch with a report of what they had seen in Victoria.

That was. . . . He pushed the befuddling thought away. It didn't matter when Will had left. All that mattered was that he push on, stay on the *Nermernuh*'s heels as ordered.

Sands lifted the reins from the bay's neck and nudged him forward toward the salty smell of the sea.

Gunshots, war cries, and screams! Together they rose as a grotesque chorus that floated on the hot gulf breeze blowing from the east.

Blowing from Linnville!

Sands spurred his borrowed bay forward in an easy gallop as he reined directly to the south. If Buffalo Hump's *Pehnahterkuhs* had reached the small settlement, he no longer had to worry about rear scouting parties—the braves now directed their full attention to fighting.

However, he had no intention of riding straight into Linnville. Bone-weary though he was, he still had wits enough about him to shy away from committing suicide.

To the south of the bay town was a long stretch of sandy beach. The rolling dunes there would provide the cover he needed for moving in close without being detected—if the Comanche weren't already on the beach.

A half mile to the south, he broke from a tangled patch of entwined underbrush. Before him stretched Lavaca Bay, and beyond, the Gulf of Mexico. In gently breaking whitecaps, the sea swelled and rolled against the shore with foamy fingers that ran up the white beach.

Here, too, were slender palms with thick frondy tops and white gulls soaring wide-winged over the peaceful bay. For a man grown accustomed to the rugged terrain of the hill country, the sun-sparkling bay was like some virgin tropical paradise.

Sands gave the beauty of the sweeping panorama no more than a cursory glance. He smiled: the beach was barren—without a trace of a single Comanche. The second thing he saw was a swelling dune that rose eight feet into the air. He rode to the base of the dune, dropped to the ground, and belly crawled to the sandy crest.

Even without his telescope, he could see closely clumped, white-washed buildings of Linnville. The tiny community lay no more than a quarter of a mile up the coastline—and it was aswarm with Comanches. Fire already licked at two of Linnville's twenty homes.

The *Pehnahterkuh*'s attention, however, was held by a small fleet of boats that rode the gently rising waves just beyond arrow and rifle range. In those boats were the citizens of Linnville, staring on in terror as Indians reined and ran through the streets of their settlement like a tidal wave come from the plains.

Sands pulled the telescope from his belt and extended its three cylindrical sections. Eyepiece to his right eye, he scanned the flotilla of small craft.

Nothing! Damnit! He didn't recognize a face on any of the boats, nor could he find the one searched for—Marion's.

Pulling the telescope away, Sands wiped at his eyes, hoping it was merely his weariness that hid Marion from him. Then he lifted the spyglass once more and peered back at the boats.

The faces were all strange to him; he couldn't even find Jamie or . . . *Wait!* There in a dingy bearing the name Maryjo, he saw Arlan Turner, Marion's fleece-haired father. But where were Marion and Jamie?

Sands searched the six faces of the Maryjo's occupants. None of them belonged to either Marion or Jamie. He shifted the telescope to a three-person sailboat beside the dingy. Still nothing.

Four boats later, he found Jamie's small face. The boy lay clutched in the arms of a gray-haired matron Sands had never seen before. Again the faces he saw did not belong to Marion. Nor could he find her among any of the boats.

Ice stabbed at his chest. What if she hadn't managed to make it to the security of the small crafts?

Sands' telescope swung back to Linnville and the howling horde that now abandoned hope of reaching the boats and their occupants and turned their attention to Linnville's homes and buildings. Amid that mass of coppery-red skin he found no hint of white, only red.

If Marion hadn't made it to the water . . . Sands refused to consider the possibility as he stared through the brass spyglass. Arlan and Jamie had made it to safety—she had, too! She had to!

Unlike Victoria, Linnville showed no signs of massacre. There were no arrow-pierced and mutilated bodies laying beneath the summer sun. Nor was there slaughtered livestock scattered around the town. From all indications, the settlement had received enough warning of the Comanche invasion to seek refuge in their miniature armada. A fact that began to melt the terrifying coldness in his heart.

Marion has to be in those boats! I just can't see her, Sands reassured himself.

The *Pehnahterkuh* might have found few victims for their arrows and lances in the port settlement, but while Sands stared on, they discovered an unexpected cache of the white man's treasure—Linn's warehouse.

The great doors to the long, wooden structure were thrown open and the Comanche poured in. Within minutes braves, squaws, and children alike were carrying off armloads of booty. Here Sands saw three squaws fighting over a bolt of red cloth. There he stared on as warriors rode through the town with stovepipe hats adorning their heads. Others paraded about beneath umbrellas and women's parasols.

Pots, pans, silver, gold, barrel hoops, cloth goods, shoes, ammunition, ladies' finery, longjohns, rifles came flowing from the warehouse in a steady stream. Within mere minutes the Comanches emptied the building's two-year store of merchandise—riches the *Pehnahterkuh* had never dreamed of were suddenly theirs.

And among that wealth within Linn's warehouse—a woman!

Sands' temples pounded as he focused on the red-haired woman who struggled to free herself from the two braves dragging her from the warehouse.

Even at this distance, Sands recognized the flaming hair and the delicate features of her terrified face. It was Marion! Unable to make good an escape to the boats, she had apparently taken refuge in the warehouse, hiding herself among the boxes and crates. Now she was once again at the mercy of the Comanche, and the *Nermernuh* had no concept of the word mercy!

Images of Carolina Davis staked naked to the ground, her white flesh slashed by hunting knives filled Sands brain. Marion's face and flawless body superimposed over that agonizing image. Unlike Carolina and her husband, Marion didn't face five braves: Buffalo Hump's whole damned army surrounded her. For Marion there would be no rescuers riding out of the night with Colts ablaze.

If she were to be saved, it had to be now while the *Pehnahterkuh* were pre-occupied with the treasures stolen from Linn's despoiled warehouse. Sands swung the telescope to the boats. They weren't that far offshore. All he had to do was ride down the braves holding Marion; once she was free they could ride into the surf and swim for the boats.

Sands knew the Comanche would see him, but surprise would be on his side. If he rode hard and fast, it just might work! It had to work—it was the only chance Marion had!

Sliding down the dune, Sands grabbed up his mount's reins and tossed them around the horse's neck. Within a heartbeat, he was in the saddle with his Colt firmly clutched in his right hand. His boots swung out then jerked down to dig spurs into the bay's flanks.

The horse lurched forward in a dead run—for two strides. An awful sound of snapping bone echoed in Sands' ears, and he knew instantly the sandy beach had taken a deadly toll—one of the bay horse's shins had given way, broken!

Kicking his boots free of the stirrups, Sands pushed from the saddle. His action came a second too late. The bay went down in a head-over-heels somersault, throwing his rider forward.

Through a grainy curtain of flying sand, Sands saw the twisted log of driftwood he hurled toward. There was a burning instant of agony as pain lanced through his skull—then the maelstrom of darkness that sucked him down into oblivion.

★SEVENTEEN★

Cool and wet—the soothing touch of a damp cloth on his forehead drew Sands out of the yawning well of unconsciousness. His eyes opened and blinked against the harshness of flickering torches.

His body went rigid for a heart-pounding instant, then relief suffused him. The faces beneath those torches were white, not red.

"Hoped to give you a mite more hospitality than this when you came visiting," a voice came from beside Sands, who turned to stare up into the face of Arlan Turner. "But I'm afraid the Comanches didn't leave much more than what you can see."

Comanches? What is he talking . . . Buffalo Hump—Linnville—the boats—John Linn's warehouse—Marion—his horse—the driftwood—they came cascading back into his head like a horrible nightmare.

Ignoring the bass drum thumping in his head, Sands pushed to his elbows and stared beyond the faces peering down on him. The darkness outside the glow of the torches was night, and the flapping sound above his head came from a makeshift tent of sailcloth. The acrid, smoldering effluvium that filled his nostrils told him what the night cloaked—Linnville was no more! Buffalo Hump's *Pehnahterkuh* had burned it to the ground before continuing on their bloody trail.

"Some of the womenfolk found you on the beach while they were gathering shellfish this evening," Arlan continued. "Your horse had broken its left shin. Had to shoot it, but we kept the bridle and saddle." He patted a pile of tack at his side.

"Marion? I saw saw two braves dragging her from the warehouse."

"Last I saw she was alive. Mrs. Watts, too . . . they took her from the customs office," Arlan said. "They didn't kill her like they did the others—three whites and two slaves—which I take to be a good sign."

"It is . . . it is," Sands slowly nodded, suddenly aware that he had lost Marion for a second time. The Comanches, what they had done with her, how they now used her, didn't matter. God willing, if he were given a third chance, he wouldn't lose her again! "What time is it? I need a horse . . . I've got to go after her . . . after Buffalo Hump!"

" 'Bout midnight the way I make. You've had yourself a nice, long rest while my men've ridden their butts off."

Sands' head jerked around to find the voice's owner—Ben McCulloch. The ranger captain from Gonzales grinned.

"Horses are in short supply. We ride one per man," this from Will Brown standing at McCulloch's side. "However, we did pick up a mule that seems to be saddle broke."

Sands grinned up at his friend. "If I can ride it, a mule will be just fine."

"Better be, 'cause Will's right. Horses are the one thing we don't have," McCulloch said, explaining he now rode with a troop of a hundred twenty men. "Most of them joined up in Victoria. They're bone tired and so are their horses, but we're on Buffalo Hump's red ass and we're going to stay there. If he's about to do what I think he is, then all we need is a few more days and we'll have all of Texas waiting for him."

McCulloch paused and stretched his arms high above his head. "Which is neither here nor there right now. We'll know better in the morning. At the moment what I need is a few hours sleep. We'll head out at sun up. S'pect you'd better grab some more shut-eye, too. Soon as Owens' troop joins up with us, the only sleep anyone's going to get is in the saddle."

"At sun up, then," Sands answered, and watched McCulloch and Will leave the makeshift tent. He turned back to Arlan. "Is Jamie all right?"

"Best as can be expected," the white-haired man answered. "Misses his mother, but he's unharmed. Tye Hawkins and his missus are looking after him tonight."

"Good," Sands said with another nod as his thoughts returned to Marion and the Comanches who attended her this night.

A few more days, McCulloch says, Sands thought, only a few days and . . . he pushed the speculation from his mind. Anything could happen in a few days, especially when Comanches were involved. Whether Marion survived now rested in more powerful hands than his own. All he could do was pray to those hands, asking them to shelter her.

"I suspect Captain McCulloch was right. You need to rest," Arlan said as he walked to the open end of the sailcloth tent. "I'll see you in the morning 'fore you ride out."

"In the morning," Sands repeated as the man left.

Laying back in the darkness, he closed his eyes and

fought his way through a barrage of visions—all focused on Marion and the braves dragging her from the warehouse—to eventually find his way to a restless sleep.

Mid-morning of August tenth, McCulloch found the Owens' troop waiting along a willow-lined creek that ran into the Colorado River a few miles to the south. The new men and horses were far from being fresh in Sands' eyes. They had ridden as long and as hard as McCulloch's men.

If Ben McCulloch was disappointed by their condition, Sands couldn't find it in his expression. His smile was one of relief: the sixty additional men swelled his original twenty-four to a troop of a hundred eighty. Texas was beginning to answer the call his riders carried forth four days ago.

While the horses were watered and were given a breather, McCulloch called the men together: "I'm not certain why he's doing it, but Buffalo Hump is acting contrary to everything I know about the Comanches . . ."

Sands silently agreed. After such a bountiful raid as the one on Linnville, the *Pehnahterkuh* ordinarily would have split their war party into a myriad of small bands, then ridden hard and fast back to the relative security of the prairie. Each of those bands would have taken a different trail to confuse any pursuers.

Buffalo Hump and his army hadn't done that. From all indications the war chief was now trying to avoid confrontation with his *Tejanos* enemies, preferring to keep his warriors in a tight ring about the immense herd of stolen horses and mules.

". . . perhaps Buffalo Hump feels his medicine's great, or maybe he doesn't want to cast away all the loot he stole from Linn's warehouse. Whatever, he's decided to make a retreat along the Colorado River. And that's where he's made his mistake. He doesn't know it yet, but we've got him now, boys. By damn, I do believe, we've got him!''

McCulloch reached up and broke a twig from an overhanging willow, then squatted on the heels of his boots in the creek's moist soil. He drew a rough serpentine line in the dirt to represent the Colorado.

"This here's the San Marcos River," he said while he drew another line then added a smaller line that he dubbed Plum Creek, a tributary of the San Marcos. Next he scratched an "X" in the dirt. "Right here, near Plum Creek, Buffalo Hump's got to cross Big Prairie. And that's where we'll get him."

Sands saw the simplicity of McCulloch's strategy. If Buffalo Hump had retreated along the path he had taken into settled Texas, there would have been no way to stop the *Pehnahterkuh* army. But the war chief now led his column through the most heavily populated region of the republic. That meant a Texian force could meet the Comanches head-on at Plum Creek . . . if enough men could be raised in time.

"I don't know if the fights gone out of Buffalo Hump's bucks or if he's losing control of his warriors, but they ain't raiding like they were on the way to the coast. They're staying in close to all the horses they've stolen," McCulloch continued. "Which means its time for us to start nipping at their heels. Letting him know we're here."

McCulloch quickly outlined his plans for his men. They would constantly harass the Comanche column, day and night.

"You'll keep Buffalo Hump on the move that way. Never give him a chance to make camp and rest," McCulloch continued. "Ride in, fire a few shots, then get the hell out. Wait a bit and another group will do the same. I want him to know you're here. Make him think that if he stops to scratch his butt, you'll run over that red ass."

"You keep saying '*you*,' Ben," one of the men from Victoria said. "You ain't thinkin' of lightin' out and leaving us, are you?"

"Not exactly," McCulloch answered with a shake of his head. "But I am leaving. I plan to ride around the *Pehnahterkuh*. There's a passel of settlements through the area above Plum Creek—enough to raise the men for a small army. I intend to have them waiting at Big Prairie."

McCulloch stood and let his gaze wander over the faces of his men. "Any questions?"

Every man stood silently.

"Good! Now let's give them a dose of their own medicine!"

★ EIGHTEEN ★

The dawn of August twelfth rose hot and muggy over Big Prairie on Plum Creek. In spite of two days' hard riding on the back of a black mule with no more than catnaps stolen between the constant harassing raids on Buffalo Hump's flank, Sands felt wide awake and alert.

Adrenaline pumped through his veins and his heart pounded in his chest to echo up to his ears like a runaway bass drum. The reason—battle lay but minutes away.

His head turned to the right and then the left. For as far as he could see in both directions stood a line of mounted Texians. Their rifles stood primed and ready with hammers cocked.

Across the grassy expanse of Big Prairie, hidden in the underbrush and trees, was another line of buckskin-clad men with loaded weapons in hand, awaiting their commanders' signals. On those signals the two parallel lines of riders would move from the dense vegetation onto the clearing known as Big Prairie—and there face the *Pehnahterkuh*.

McCulloch had promised that Texas would answer the call to arms, and it had. John Moore, Edward Burleson, and Big Foot Wallace were there and with them their ranger commands. Here, too, was the Bastrop Militia.

Even Matthew Caldwell, who had been wounded in the leg during the Council House Fight, was here, fully recovered from his rifle wound, with his patrol beside him. Caldwell and McCulloch were now positioned beside Brigadier General Felix Huston, who was nominally in command of the amassed army, three riders from Sands. He could hear the three whispering their last minute plans and speculations for the forthcoming battle.

Sands hadn't believed the reports that the messenger brought last night with orders for McCulloch's men to circle the Comanche and regroup around Big Prairie. He even had found it hard to accept when he saw the steady stream of men who had flowed into the bushy bottom lands through the night. Only now did he truly accept what his eyes perceived.

In a mere six days, Texas had raised an army—an army of every able-bodied man who could sit a saddle and wield a rifle. From Gonzales, Victoria, Austin, Lavaca, Cuero, and score upon score of small communities and settlements, they had rallied to the call.

Sands' chest swelled with pride. To be certain there were men who had faced the Comanches before, but for the most part the men gathered here had never lifted a gun in battle. Today they would face a trial by fire.

Even the Tonkawa chief Placido, with fourteen warriors, had run thirty miles to join the Texians in their battle against the Comanche. Placido and his braves—still on foot because of the shortage of horses and with white rags tied to their arms so that their white allies could distinguish them from Comanches when the fighting began—now served as scouts for General Huston.

Sands' head turned from the line of mounted men, and he stared at the cloud of dust that billowed in the air to the south. The *Pehnahterkuh* approached, unaware of the mounted force awaiting them.

Once Buffalo Hump had committed himself to a route along the Colorado River, McCulloch had outguessed the war chief every step of the way. And with each of those steps, McCulloch's men had harassed the Comanche column, driving them northward toward Plum Creek. When the men's horses collapsed and died from exhaustion, they continued on foot or on mustangs stolen from the *Nermernuh*, never stopping as they nipped at Buffalo Hump's heels.

And now the rewards of those two days of ceaseless hit-and-run fighting was about to pay off. Within minutes the Comanche would be on Big Prairie.

As Sands stared at the approaching column he could see the effects of McCulloch's strategy. The Comanche were totally unprepared for combat. Except for a few braves positioned as outriders along the massive band of *Pehnahterkuh*, the warriors were scattered through the herd of stolen horses and mules. Their full attention was on the livestock—animals grown cantankerous and tired from the constant press.

"Check your weapons," a rider whispered beside Sands.

Sands did as ordered and passed the command to Will on his left. He then looked back at Buffalo Hump's army as it moved onto Big Prairie.

"Forward!" this from General Huston.

A similiar command echoed from across the grassy flatlands.

There was no chaotic charge, no mad scramble out of the heavy foliage. Nor was there the blaring chorus of trumpeted bugles to announce the attack. Deadly silent and with faces set in cool determination the two parallel lines of mounted Texians *walked* their mounts onto Big Prairie in an almost leisurely pace and converged on the marching *Pehnahterkuh*.

Had his mind not been set with the grim task before him, Sands would have laughed at the ludicrous scene that met the Texian army. Many of the *Nermernuh* still wore the spoils of the Linnville raid. Black stovepipe hats adorned countless warriors' heads. Here and there braves, many in buffalo-horned headdress, had spread umbrellas and parasols to shade them from the harsh August sun, presenting a grotesque mingling of savage ferocity and the ridiculous. Even their ponies' tails and manes were tied with long ribbons of red cloth.

Secure in the belief that Buffalo Hump's powerful medicine had made the band invulnerable, the Comanche outriders galloped up and down the column, almost prancing and preening. Without the slightest hint of fear, they taunted the line of *Tejanos*, while performing riding tricks on the backs of their mustangs that reminded Sands of circus acrobats and their daring stunts. The challenges for the whites to ride forth and face them in hand-to-hand combat were wasted on the Texians; the majority had never heard Comanche before.

Sands strained, trying to find Marion amid the motley column of Indians. All he saw was Comanches, horses, mules, Comanches, and more Comanches. His heart quickened its pace. *Have they killed her?*

No! he answered himself. Marion was still alive. McCulloch's men had pressed the horde too hard for two days. Buffalo Hump's followers hadn't been given the time to torture prisoners. And if the Comanches had killed her quickly with a arrow or a rifle ball, the body would have been found.

Marion's still alive. All I have to do is find her! Somehow. Somehow!

"They're putting on a show to delay us, General," Sands heard Matthew Caldwell call to Huston. "They want to get the horses and mules by before we attack. Now's the time to move! Signal the charge!"

Caldwell was right, Sands realized. The acrobatic outriders could never stop a mounted charge; their fantastic display of horsemanship was performed simply to dazzle the *Tejanos*. Ninety percent of Buffalo Hump's warriors remained amid the massive herd of horses and mules, unable to maneuver their ponies, let alone help defend the band.

Huston merely sat, watching the *Pehnahterkuh* column as though he hadn't heard the ranger captain.

The Indians grew bolder, riding closer and closer to the lines of buckskin-clad soldiers to shout their insults and challenges. A long and lanky warrior, with a streaming feathered war bonnet atop his head, rode out of the main column. The brave was too tall for a Comanche. Sands pegged him for a Kiowa, a northern tribe who often allied themselves with the stronger and more vicious *Nermernuh* bands.

With only coup stick in hand, the warrior rode straight at the mounted lines and drew his chestnut pony to an abrupt halt ten yards from General Huston. In the Comanche tongue, he derided the parental lineage of his white enemies and their lack of courage. He challenged the whole army, saying he would face them one by one in single combat.

The Kiowa brave was either extremely brave or extremely insane, Sands decided as he stared into the shouting red face with its streaks of crimson and black war paint.

Only Caldwell reacted to the warrior's challenge. The

ranger captain turned to the man mounted beside him and simply said, "Shoot him."

The rider, a man Sands recognized as being among those who joined McCulloch in Victoria, lifted his long rifle, sighted, and squeezed the trigger. The report sounded as though a heavy branch had cracked in two.

The Kiowa jerked, then his body went rigid. A dark purple hole had opened in the center of his forehead. Sands saw his eyes, wide and round, and a befuddled expression of disbelief shadowing his face just before he tumbled to the ground—dead.

A moan, rising from deep in the chest and pushing itself hoarsely through the throat, worked its way over Comanche lips as Buffalo Hump's warriors stared on in confusion. If they had felt the war chief's medicine would protect them, a single rifle ball had dispelled that belief. For such a brave warrior, even one who was a lowly Kiowa, to be killed so easily was bad medicine.

"Damnit, man! Charge!" Caldwell demanded. "Charge 'em, General!"

This time Huston came to life. With his rifle raised high, he shouted a single word, *"Charge!"*

Every Texian answered by lifting his rifle and firing it into the Comanche column. In the next instant, a blood-chilling scream that mimicked the *Nermernuh*'s own war cries tore from the throats of the white soldiers—and they charged.

Sands yanked his Colt from his belt as he slid his now useless one-shot rifle into its holster on the saddle. He took aim at one of the nearby Comanche outriders and fired. The brave's hands grasped at his chest as he fell from the back of his mustang.

Without taking time to aim, Sands swung the pistol to another brave, pointed its barrel and fired. Like the first, this warrior slid from his pony, hit the ground, and lay there, as dead as the Kiowa whose death had begun the charge.

"Son of a bitch!" Will cursed at Sands' side.

The ranger jerked around to see his friend break off a Comanche arrow that jutted from his thigh. Will's sun-browned face was as white as a bleached sheet, and pain contorted his youthful features—but he rode on, his Colt once more rising to spit lead into the Comanche horde.

When Sands' head turned back to the outriders, they were gone—all killed by the double wave of howling Texians who crashed upon them from two sides. The few skirmish fighters Buffalo Hump had positioned about the main column of his army had died quick and clean.

The same could not be said for the *Nermernuh* who died now.

The Texian army thundered headlong into the main column of Comanches. The rifle and pistol shots and the ceaseless cries of the buckskinned riders took a natural toll—the horses and mules stampeded!

And in that instant the battle was won.

Mules overloaded with the spoils of John Linn's warehouse lunged forward in a dead run, only to plunge into the boggy ground around Plum Creek. The pile up equalled that of a derailed locomotive as animal ran atop animal atop animal. And then the horses came, pounding into mules.

Amid all were the *Pehnahterkuh*. Those on foot went down beneath sharp hooves, their death cries drowned by the rolling reports of the Texians' guns. Braves, squaws, and children were caught in the deadly tide of horseflesh.

The mounted warriors were no better prepared to meet the unexpected stampede. Unable to rein their ponies free of the panicked animals, they fell: some thrown from their mounts, others cut down by the hail of bullets that showered the struggling mass of man and animal.

And still Sands and the rest of the Texian army charged, pressing the terror-panicked animals into a fevered frenzy as they sought to escape the thundering guns.

Warriors who somehow managed to remain astride their mounts, now abandoned the mustangs and ran—leaping from back to lathered back across the great herd of stolen animals. Immediately companies of rangers broke from the charge and pursued the fleeing Comanches into the heavy woods surrounding Big Prairie.

"Josh! There!" Will called out.

Sands' head twisted around. His young friend pointed across the boiling mass of man and animal. *Marion!*

There, slung across a dappled gray like a sack of potatoes, was the woman he loved. With her on the bolting horse was a Comanche brave, his dark, braided hair streaming in the air behind him. As Sands watched in mute agony, the brave, the horse, and Marion disappeared into the coastal forest.

Without another glance to the now dispersed column of Comanches, Sands reined the mule he still rode toward the trees, and dug his spurs into its dark flanks.

★ NINETEEN ★

Silence—unnatural silence pressed around Sands as he eased back on the reins and drew the mule to a halt. Big Prairie was but a quarter of a mile behind him, yet the battle sounds no longer penetrated the dense vegetation.

Nor did any other sound.

He cocked his head, listening. Nothing touched his ears, not even the hum of insects buzzing in the summer heat.

Cautiously, he pulled back the hammer to his Colt. The two metallic clicks as it cocked resounded through the preternatural stillness. Still there was no answer from the wood—no bird on fluttering wings, no startled jackrabbit fleeing at his approach—only silence.

Sands nudged the mule forward in a slow walk. The brave was here waiting—he could feel him. His steel-blue eyes rolled to the branches overhead for an instant. Nothing. Was he behind the oak ahead? Sands' gaze shifted to the right as the mule lumbered by the ancient bole. Nothing. That dense canebrake to the left? Nothing.

A glint of sunlight on metal! He saw it out of the corner of his eye amid a bushy growth of honeysuckle just beyond the oak on his right.

Sands reacted rather than thought. He lunged to the left,

throwing himself from the saddle. He felt the swish of air on the back of his neck as a razor-honed war lance speared empty air.

Then he hit the ground—hard. Harder than he had anticipated. His roll came a fraction of a second too late. He struck the grassy forest floor and just lay there, his shoulder throbbing in pain. And his Colt?

He didn't know. The impact jarred it from his grip; his hand now surrounded hot, muggy air.

The sound of rushing footsteps brought him to life. Sands flipped to his back and stared up into a war-painted face and the wicked head of a lance meant to impale his chest.

Again the ranger reacted. Both his arms flew up, hands grasping the lance shaft behind the feather and ribbon decorated head. He jerked to the left, then down.

The lance thrusted deep into the loamy soil a fraction of an inch from Sands' side. The warrior, holding tight to his weapon, vaulted through the air and hit the ground in a somersaulting roll.

The moment of confusion was all that was needed for Sands to scramble to his feet. A hasty glance told him what he already knew, the Colt was lost in the high grass and there wasn't time to find it. His hand dropped to the sheath slung on his belt; steel on leather hissed as he yanked his hunting knife free.

Before he could take advantage of the brave's tumbling spill, the Comanche warrior sprang to his feet. In his hand—his own deadly blade.

"I will cut away your shriveled manhood and feed it to the ants!" the brave spat in his native tongue as his jet black eyes coolly glared at Sands. "Your scalp will hang from my war lance!"

"And I'll piss on your grave!" Sands said as he lunged

forward, his blade slicing upward toward the brave's naked belly.

The Comanche didn't backstep as he had anticipated. Instead his arm whipped out, a powerful grip encircling the ranger's wrist. Simultaneously, the warrior lashed out, his blade meant to open Sands' throat from ear to ear.

Sands ducked beneath the whistling knife, and launched himself forward. With the full weight of his body behind it, his head rammed into the Comanche's solar plexus. Air rushed from the warrior's lungs in an astonished "oouuff!"

In that moment of surprise, Sands felt the vise-tight fingers about his wrist slacken. The warrior's single heartbeat of disorientation provided the opening he needed.

As ranger and Comanche tumbled to the ground, Sands wrenched his hand from the confining grip. In a fluid follow through, he thrusted the long knife inward. He felt the brief resistance as the steel tip met bone, then slipped upward a quarter of an inch to slide easily between two ribs and drive straight to the heart.

The brave's dark eyes flew wide to stare with incomprehension into the face of the ranger laying on top of him. A throaty, moist rattle gurgled from his quivering lips just before his body went totally flaccid as the last delicate threads of life frayed and snapped.

Temples apound and knees watery weak, Sands shoved himself from the still body. He lay on his back staring at the leafy canopy of boughs above while he gulped down breath after breath. That had been closer than he liked. If he hadn't caught the glint of sunlight on the lance head . . .

He pushed the thought away. There was no sense in dwelling on what might have been. What mattered was that he had seen the glint and his blade had been surer than the brave's. He was alive and the enemy he had faced was dead. It was a harsh and cruel judgment of what had transpired here in the heart of this coastal forest, but it was all that carried any weight in an untamed land such as Texas. Perhaps one day men would be able to live their lives by loftier codes: this day survival and survival alone ruled.

Sands pushed to his elbows and glanced around. His black mule stood twenty feet away idly munching grass around the bit in its mouth. A humorless irony touched the ranger's lips as he started to rise. There in the grass, no more than an inch from his fingertips lay his lost Colt. He shook his head as he retrieved the weapon, carefully uncocked it, and tucked the barrel into his belt.

Turning to the dead brave, he reached down, pulled his blade from the Comanche's unmoving chest, and wiped away the blood on the grass before slipping it back into its leather sheath.

A rustle of underbrush brought the Colt from Sands' belt. His thumb jerked back the hammer as he swirled. Nothing! There was no Comanche to face him, no lance or knife poised to rob his life.

The rustle came again—from beyond the vining honeysuckle that had concealed the brave.

Picking his way around the thick, dangled growth, he entered a tiny clearing. There, tightly bound to the trunk of a sweetgum tree, with a swath of red cloth gagging her mouth, was Marion. The rustling sound came from a dead branch she nudged with the toe or her foot.

Her emerald green eyes rose to meet his with a mingled gaze of exhaustion, relief, and joy.

Once again, Sands returned his pistol to his belt and freed the hunting knife. In two long strides, he was at the tree, the sharp blade severing the cords that bound Marion's body to the bole.

"He was going to kill me!" Marion said as she pulled

the red cloth from her mouth. "He had the lance raised when he heard you approach. He . . ."

Sands' mouth covered hers, muffling the rest of her words. He pulled her to him and held her there tightly. Too many months had passed since he had last savored the feel of this magnificent woman—months lost because of his own stupidity and prejudice. Now, he had been given a third chance—this time he intended to keep her just where she was!

★TWENTY★

Blood Moon, the sound of it in Sands' mind was strange and alien here and now. The rugged hill country seemed as far away from the Gulf of Mexico as did the full moon that hung overhead. *How a month can change things!*

Sands stretched out in the cool grass skirting the white beach, and let the gentle night breeze dry the drops of water clinging to his naked body. The sound of banjo, guitar, and fiddle playing a lively rendition of "Cumberland Gap" drifted up from Indianola on the warm southerly breeze, barely audible above the breaking surf of Lavaca Bay.

They'll be dancing 'till sun up, Sands thought. A self-satisfied smile moved across his lips, as he remembered the hoedown Marion and he had left two hours ago.

He still wasn't certain why the townsfolk in the community positioned on the south shore of Lavaca Bay had been celebrating, but it didn't matter, most people didn't need much of an excuse for breaking out a fiddle and playing a tune. All that really mattered was that the music was good, the food bountiful, and the liquor flowing. The shindig in Indianola had provided all three. The fifteen-mile drive from Linnville had been well worth it.

Sands' gaze shifted back to the moonlit bay and Marion who still frolicked in the breaking waves like some mythological mermaid. They had driven only half the way back to Linnville before she had suggested the moonlight swim. Stripping away their clothes they had plunged into the gulf.

Their swim had been brief. Within minutes they found themselves back on shore, rolling in each other's arms. The fierce hunger of Marion's lovemaking still lingered in Sands' mind. There was a desperation in the rhythm of her body he had never felt before. However, when their desires had been sated, Marion had pulled him back into the sea before he could question her puzzling behavior.

Sands' gaze moved northward. The few flickering lights of Linnville could be seen from his position. It was hard to imagine the Comanche horde that had razed the small community a month ago. A few of Linnville's residents had moved south to Indianola after the Comanche raid. But the majority had remained and rebuilt the town. Already fresh stores lay in John Linn's new warehouse.

Even the battle of Plum Creek seemed to be part of a past—centuries away. Here beside the peaceful bay with its palms and warm breeze, Sands found it difficult to remember the bloody horror of the stampeding horses and mules. Or the long pursuit as the Texian army had divided and chased the escaping bands of Comanches back to the plains.

Only one Texian had been killed in the battle, while General Huston had estimated that Buffalo Hump had lost a quarter of his warriors at Big Prairie. As with the squaws taken after the Council House Fight, the prisoners had not been killed, but parceled out as "servants." Already many of these "servants" had escaped back to *Pehnahterkuh* lands on the backs of stolen horses.

As for the booty taken by the Comanche during their six days of terror, it had been divided among the men who fought at Plum Creek. Most of the men who answered the rangers' call for help had gone home wealthier than when they first arrived in the marshy bottom lands.

Sands' share had been twenty head of horses and mules. These he had sold for a nice profit—one he intended to use to purchase a small farm outside Linnville—as soon as Marion answered the question he had proposed while they danced at Indianola this night.

A squirming disquiet wiggled through Sands as he remembered the furrows that had briefly wrinkled Marion's brow when he had asked her to marry him. The hugging arms and wet smacking kisses he had expected had not come in answer to that all important question. Instead, Marion had said she needed to talk with him before "committing" herself.

Sands still waited for her answer—and that "talk."

He looked back to the gulf. Unashamed of her nakedness, Marion walked from the foamy surf and trotted toward him. The moonlight played on the water clinging to her sleek form, igniting the droplets like a million sparkling gems. The same drops that sprinkled coolly over his dry skin as she lowered herself to the grass beside him.

"It's so beautiful here," she said as her gaze wandered over the bay. "I feel so alive and part of it, like some pagan lost in her worship of nature."

Sands grinned. "If the people back at the hoedown in Indianola saw you now, they'd agree!"

The smile that touched Marion's lips was a weak attempt at a laugh. No sound moved over her lips. She merely glanced at him, then looked back at the surf.

"Pa told me you rejoined the rangers today," she said softly.

"There's rumors of Santa Anna sending another army up from Mexico. The rangers are looking for men, just in case," Sands answered. "Since Will's leg's healed, we rode into Victoria and signed up."

"Is that what you want, Josh? To be a ranger again?" Marion turned to him. He could see the intense expression on her delicate face through the shadows cast by the moon.

"It's the only thing I know," he shrugged. Something within him went hollow and sinking. Marion was looking for an answer; what it was, he wasn't sure. However, he sensed that his words had been the wrong ones. "I'm good at what I do."

"Some men farm the land. Some men are merchants. Others build wagons or shoe horses. And some men are rangers," Marion's voice grew even lower. "And everyone of them is needed—all have their jobs to be done. But ranging is more than a job to you, isn't it?"

Sands' sinking feeling increased. "I guess that's one way of looking at it. A man's got to do what he's cut out to do. As long as the Comanche ride and as long as there's a threat of the Mexican Army invading the republic, there'll be a need for rangers. One day this country will be as peaceful as it was back in Ohio, but that's still a way off as I see it."

Marion sat quietly, staring back at the gulf. Sands could almost hear her thinking, but he could not sense the direction of those thoughts.

"I've been trying to avoid this, hoping against hope that there would never be a need for me to face what I've been fearing ever since you found me," she finally said with a sudden firmness in her voice. "But a woman's like a man, she's got to do what she's got to do."

Marion's head slowly turned to him and she reached out and took his hand. "After what I'm about to say you may find this hard to believe, but I love you, Josh Sands . . . perhaps more than I've ever loved any man."

"Marion, I love you. I've told you and tried to show what I feel." How easy the words came now to him; how right and natural they sounded.

"I know, and that's what makes what I have to say . . . have to do . . . so hard," she continued. "And though everything within me is crying out for me to say 'yes, I'll marry you . . . happily spend the rest of our lives together,' I can't."

"Can't?"

"Can't," she repeated. "Because I'm not certain there will be a rest of your life. Everytime you would ride out on patrol, there would be the possibility that you wouldn't return. Someday Will would come knocking at our door, holding his hat in his hands with his big eyes all sad and downcast. He'll stutter and stammer a bit, then he'll blurt out that you didn't ride back from patrol this time—that you were killed by a Comanche arrow or a Mexican bullet. I couldn't live with that—not the long sleepless nights of not knowing, always waiting for Will to come to our door. I've had one husband taken from me. I'm not strong enough to endure losing another."

Sands tried to find the words to reassure her—but there were none. She was right. There was nothing certain about a ranger's life—especially the prospect of living to a ripe old age.

"I could quit ranging—quit it for good. I've been thinking about using the money I got from selling the horses to buy us a small spread. It wouldn't be much to start with, but I could grow tobacco and maybe some cotton. It would grow, I know it would. In time . . ."

Marion's warm lips lightly pressed to his, hushing him.

When she eased back, her head moved sadly from side to side.

"Another woman might believe Josh Sands could lay aside his rifle and pistol and take up farming, but I'm not another woman. I know what ranging means to you. You might work the land for a year or two, but down deep inside it would be killing you. You'd be aching for the patrols and the open country of the frontier."

She paused, her hand squeezing his tightly. "Like as not I'd wake up one morning, and you'd be gone. And you'd never be back. Or worse, you'd stay on out of a sense of obligation and duty, but you'd hate it. And you'd end up hating me for keeping you away from the life you love."

Her eyes lifted and stared into Sands'. "Josh, I couldn't live with that either, not seeing all the love we share become some twisted ugly thing that would blacken both our hearts."

Again, Sands couldn't find the words to comfort her—once more they didn't exist. Perhaps someday in the future he might be ready to settle down and try his hand at farming. But now ranging was all he knew—all he wanted. As Marion had said there was a job to be done and he was a man who could do it.

"I guess that leaves us out in the cold," he finally found the heart within to speak.

"No, it leaves us with a lot of warm, tender feelings. It leaves us with the love we feel for one another. That's something some people never experience," she whispered, leaning over to kiss his cheek. "And that's something nobody, not even you or I, will ever be able to take away."

Sands' gaze shifted upward to the now melancholy waves lapping against the sandy beach. A shadow had fallen over the paradise he had found among the palms and the bay. That shadow was the one he cast himself.

"I guess, the only question left is, what happens now?" he said as he turned back to Marion.

"I suppose you and Will will ride out of Linnville in the morning and go wherever the rangers need you. But that's in the morning," she answered. "As for *now*, there's still a long time before dawn, and there's no one here but you and me. I don't want to waste a second of that time."

Sands replied by scooping her lithe form into his arms and hungrily pressing his mouth to hers. A wise man had once written that a single night spent in loving could be a lifetime unto itself. He intended to make certain Marion and he shared a rich and full life this night.

Watch for

THE HORSE MARINES

second book in the exciting
new **THE TEXIAN** series

coming in August!

EDGE

BY
George G. Gilman

More bestselling western adventure from Pinnacle, America's #1 series publisher. Over 8 million copies of EDGE in print!

☐ 41-279-7 Loner #1	$1.75	☐ 41-837-X Savage Dawn #26	$1.95
☐ 41-868-X Ten Grand #2	$1.95	☐ 41-309-2 Death Drive #27	$1.75
☐ 41-769-1 Apache Death #3	$1.95	☐ 40-204-X Eve of Evil #28	$1.50
☐ 41-282-7 Killer's Breed #4	$1.75	☐ 41-775-6 The Living, The Dying, and The Dead #29	$1.95
☐ 41-836-1 Blood on Silver #5	$1.95	☐ 41-312-2 Towering Nightmare #30	$1.75
☐ 41-770-5 Red River #6	$1.95	☐ 41-313-0 Guilty Ones #31	$1.75
☐ 41-285-1 California Kill #7	$1.75	☐ 41-314-9 Frightened Gun #32	$1.75
☐ 41-286-X Hell's Seven #8	$1.75	☐ 41-315-7 Red Fury #33	$1.75
☐ 41-287-8 Bloody Summer #9	$1.75	☐ 41-987-2 A Ride in the Sun #34	$1.95
☐ 41-771-3 Black Vengeance #10	$1.95	☐ 41-776-4 Death Deal #35	$1.95
☐ 41-289-4 Sioux Uprising #11	$1.75	☐ 41-448-X Vengeance at Ventura #37	$1.75
☐ 41-290-8 Death's Bounty #12	$1.75	☐ 41-449-8 Massacre Mission #38	$1.95
☐ 41-772-1 Tiger's Gold #14	$1.95	☐ 41-450-1 The Prisoners #39	$1.95
☐ 41-293-2 Paradise Loses #15	$1.75	☐ 41-451-X Montana Melodrama #40	$2.25
☐ 41-294-0 Final Shot #16	$1.75	☐ 41-924-4 The Killing Claim #41	$2.25
☐ 41-838-8 Vengeance Valley #17	$1.95	☐ 41-106-5 Two of a Kind	$1.75
☐ 41-773-X Ten Tombstones #18	$1.95	☐ 41-894-9 Edge Meets Steele: Matching Pair	$2.25
☐ 41-297-5 Ashes and Dust #19	$1.75
☐ 41-774-8 Sullivan's Law #20	$1.95
☐ 40-487-5 Slaughter Road #22	$1.50
☐ 41-302-5 Slaughterday #24	$1.75
☐ 41-802-7 Violence Trail #25	$1.95

Buy them at your local bookstore or use this handy coupon
Clip and mail this page with your order

**PINNACLE BOOKS, INC.—Reader Service Dept.
1430 Broadway, New York, NY 10018**

Please send me the book(s) I have checked above. I am enclosing $_____ (please add 75¢ to cover postage and handling). Send check or money order only—no cash or C.O.D.'s.

Mr./Mrs./Miss _____

Address _____

City _____ State/Zip _____

Please allow six weeks for delivery. Prices subject to change without notice.

SIX-GUN SAMURAI

by Patrick Lee

FROM THE LAND OF THE SHOGUNS AND AMERICA'S #1 SERIES PUBLISHER, AN EXCITING NEW ACTION/ADVENTURE SERIES THAT COMBINES FAR-EASTERN TRADITION WITH HARDCORE WESTERN VIOLENCE!

Stranded in Japan, American-born Tom Fletcher becomes immersed in the ancient art of bushido—a violent code demanding bravery, honor and ultimate sacrifice—and returns to his homeland on a bloodsoaked trail of vengeance.

☐ 41-190-1	SIX-GUN SAMURAI #1	$1.95
☐ 41-191-X	SIX-GUN SAMURAI #2 Bushido Vengeance	$1.95
☐ 41-192-8	SIX-GUN SAMURAI #3 Gundown at Golden Gate	$1.95
☐ 41-416-1	SIX-GUN SAMURAI #4 Kamikaze Justice	$1.95
☐ 41-417-X	SIX-GUN SAMURAI #5 The Devil's Bowman	$1.95
☐ 41-418-8	SIX-GUN SAMURAI #6 Bushido Lawman	$1.95

Buy them at your local bookstore or use this handy coupon
Clip and mail this page with your order

PINNACLE BOOKS, INC.—Reader Service Dept.
1430 Broadway, New York, NY 10018

Please send me the book(s) I have checked above. I am enclosing $_____ (please add 75¢ to cover postage and handling). Send check or money order only—no cash or C.O.D.'s.

Mr./Mrs./Miss _____

Address _____

City _____ State/Zip _____

Please allow six weeks for delivery. Prices subject to change without notice.